Aurelia Yates

characters, places, and incidents either
are products of the author's imagination
or are used fictitiously. Any resemblance
to actual persons, living or dead, events,
or locales is entirely coincidental.

ISBN- 979-8-9910612-0-9

TABLE OF CONTENTS

WARNING

This book is rated R; not appropriate for readers under 18 years of age; contains elements of sex, cheating, and language.

CHAPTER 1

Colt

The engine rumbles between my legs, making the vibrations spread through me, sending an adrenaline straight rush to my fingertips. I press the throttle and my bike picks up speed, making the fresh air rush harder past in my face. Every curve on the country road, my bike handles with precision and ease. The smooth ride disintegrating all the stress in my body.

When I make my destination at the Fallen Saints Club House, I pull up and turn off the old gal. My bike has been with me since I could drive. She was a gift from my dad, a happy fifteenth birthday, you could say. We still take a ride together from time to time, but since I've opened my bar, time is something I have less off.

"Colt," Cutter says, coming up to me, embracing me in a brotherly hug. "Glad you made it. Jay watching the bar tonight?"

"Yeah, I needed a night off," I comment, exhaustion settling over me.

He laughs, "I'm guessing you haven't gotten laid in some time," he says with a wicked grin. Throwing his head back to look at Serena, who's standing a few feet away, he wiggles his eyebrows. "You know," he lowers his voice. "Serena is always down for a good time." I look over his shoulder and shudder at the thought of sticking my dick in her.

Serena's a house mouse, just another woman hanging around the club trying to suck anyone's cock that will pull it out for her. She's a beautiful woman, but too well used for my taste. There's only one woman my dick will rise for, and she's not been within arm's reach in nearly three long fucking months.

Another laugh bellows out of Cutter, bringing me out of my daydreaming.

"Fuck man. What's got your dick tucking away from her?" I try to relax the nauseated facial expression I've got plastered on my face.

He looks back over at Serena like she's a grand prize to be won. Licking his lips, he says, "Fuck, I'm already hard just thinking about how she sucked me off last weekend. She can make me blow —"

"Save it. I don't need to hear anymore about your dick," I walk off, leaving his tongue wagging, for Serena.

"Hey Colt," another house mouse purrs when I

step onto the porch to head inside. I give her a nod and keep walking.

When I open the front door, music blares, making the empty liquor bottles on the table rattle to the beat. It's packed, as it always is on a weekend night. Women walk around in barely nothing, showing more skin than they would in a bathing suit. They flow through the clubhouse hoping to snag a member. Becoming a member's old lady has perks and one of them is the respect they would get being associated with the club's name.

Grabbing a bottle of beer, I take a drink and park my ass on the couch, throwing my head back to rest my eyes. When I feel the sofa dip on both sides of my legs, I frown. It doesn't take a genius to figure out it's Serena and her friend. Serena's loud perfume fills my nostrils, making me want to gag. It's overkill.

Nails scrap up my thighs. "Colt," Serena's voice scratches at my eardrums like nails on a chalkboard.

My eyes open and I lazily look at her as my hand brushes theirs away. Serena flinches slightly at the dismissal.

"Do you like my new outfit?" She caves her shoulders in, making her tits push together. "I thought about you when I bought it."

For fuck's sake. Maybe I should take her back to my room and just fuck her. Before last summer, my dick would be eager to take part in a threesome even if it was Serena offering her pussy, but I can't seem to get him on board, no matter how hard I try.

"First, let me watch," I say, hoping to distract them.

They both plaster huge smiles on at my words. It makes my stomach roll with disgust. I give myself a pep talk. Get your mind off Maggie and get your dick wet. If the sight of these two beautiful women can't spring my dick back from its permanent vacation, I don't think there will be any hope for me in the future. I might have to invest in a pump. Oh God, just the thought makes my lip curl into a snarl. Only men in their eighties use those things. Fuck me, no way. I'll just go limp or see an erection specialist.

"Are you going to join us?" Selena asks.

I can't help but stare at her lips. It's the most unnatural set I've ever seen. With all the Botox she has had, she could suck the skin off my balls. I shiver just thinking about it. Without saying a word, I stand, extending a hand out to Serena. She places hers in mine and I lead them down the hall and around the corner to my room. My room is the last door at the end of the hall, which gives me the most privacy.

Opening my bedroom door, I stand aside, allowing them to walk past me. Their giggles make my skin crawl. How in the hell am I going to get out of this?

"Make yourselves comfortable," Extending my arm, I suggest the bed for them to sit on.

Both women sway their hips to the bed. Sitting on the edge, Serena pats the space between them, suggesting for me to sit. When I close the door behind me, I choose to ignore her suggestion and walk over to the small bar. Pulling out some whiskey, I pour myself a full glass. I'm going to need to drink myself stupid if I have to sit here and watch this.

"Is there anything you want us to do for you first?" Serena asks while licking her lips.

"No," I say sharply.

The women look at each other and then back at me. Without breaking eye contact, Selena grabs Serena's large tits through her bralette. Moaning, Serena closes her eyes, enjoying the moment, then throws her head back. When she opens them, they're blazing with heat. That's all it takes for Selena to reach up with both hands and yank Serena's top down, breaking the small straps that fall over her shoulders.

When her large breasts fall out, it makes me think of Maggie and how her bathing suit top came untied. Fuck! Her amazing tits bounced on the float with each hard wave. I wanted to wrap my lips around them.

I hear the women pawing at each other, bringing me back to the present. Good. They've forgotten all about me.

When Selena pulls Serena's shorts down and plants her face in Serena's pussy, I've had all I can take. I push myself off the wall and walk into the connected bathroom, locking the door behind me.

Closing my eyes, I lean against the door, exhaling, and bring my drink up to my lips to sip on. Swallowing the whiskey, I feel the burn blistering a trail to my stomach, making me appreciate the distraction of the shit that's happening in my bed.

"Maggie, Maggie," I shake my head. "What have you done to me?"

***

I wake up, trying to raise my heavy eyelids.

Oh fuck!

The loud pounding in my head makes me groan. I drank way too much last night. Turning my head slightly to the left, pain shoots through my body. Shit! I shouldn't have taken those last shots of tequila. Finally, my eyes open to a slit, and I have to close them again immediately. Just the slightest amount of light brings a throb to my head. I haven't been drunk like that since I was a teenager trying to cop a feel with the head cheerleader.

When I feel the burn of the tequila rising back up, I shoot out of bed and stumble my way to the bathroom, hoping to God I make it before I lose the contents threatening to come back up. When I make it in time, I regret the decision of drinking too much with each heave.

"Fuck!" I got so drunk last night thinking of Maggie and how hot she looked in that leather bikini on fourth of July. Images of her have been burned in my brain like a permanent photo book.

I heave again and wish I could just rip the photos out of my memory bank so I can move on. Maggie's very existence has invaded my mind and has control over my dick. When I finish emptying my stomach, I swipe my mouth with the back of my hand and stagger to the sink. Propping my hands on the counter, I try to hold myself from falling over because my head sways like a wind chime in a windstorm. The small mirror on the medicine cabinet in front of me reflects a man that's seen better mornings. I shake my head at the sight.

"Fuck, man, get your shit together," I whisper.

After washing up, I walk back into my room. Two women are sleeping on their backs with their tits on full display. I curse myself for not remembering much, but I'm pretty sure I didn't get laid. My dick feels dry as a bone. I reach down and check on him. Yep, dry as a fucking bone. Running my other hand through my hair, I tug at it.

"What the hell is wrong with me?" I say to no one because the bombshells that are in my bed look like they're in a coma.

I wince slightly when I remember when they tried to put their hands down my pants to pull out my dick. I wasn't even hard. It didn't matter how they licked at each other or nipped at my ears. My dick wasn't willing to take part.

One woman rolls over to her stomach, spreading her legs to give me a view of her stretched out pussy. Maybe it's good I couldn't get my dick to cooperate. That pussy looks way too over used for me.

I reach for my shirt and shoes, trying to ease out the door. I'm hoping they will leave when they notice I'm not here. Mental note, burn my bed.

When I think I'm about to escape without talking to anyone, I see Shadow standing close to my bike, smoking a cigarette. He gives me a nod and grins. He's thinking I fucked the two babes in my room. Yeah, let him think that. It's better than them knowing the truth, that I can only get it hard for one woman.

"Off to work?" Shadow says in his raspy voice.

"Yeah, got a lot of shit to do. You coming by later to finish up?"

"Be there shortly. Got to do some… stuff first." I give him a quick acknowledgement with a head tilt and get on my bike.

Shadow has been doing some construction on my bar, and he's damn good at what he does. The man knows his shit, but he's one scary mother-fucker. His past is about as shady as a whore in a back alley. I've not asked him about it, mainly because I know better. I'm in this brotherhood for the family and warm pussy. These days, I'm just in it for the brotherhood.

This group of men is a second family to me. A family that I pledged my loyalty to until my last breath. Some members may be involved in some shady, illegal shit, stealing, selling guns, and running a ring of prostitutes, but no one takes drugs. That's the rule. We don't allow our members to mess with dope. As long as I've been with the club, we have had no issues.

Kick starting my Harley, the rumble vibrates through my body, and I welcome the feeling. Pushing the throttle, I head to the bar to get some work done.

CHAPTER 2

Colt

A bang occurs, making me jump up from a deep sleep. White blurs my vision and I peel away the invoice that is stuck to the side of my face. Last night's drinking binge combined with the workload has drained me of energy.

My work in the office is a mountain of never-ending paperwork. I need an extra employee, someone to take care of the office. I just haven't set aside the time to interview anyone. The front bar has been my priority in making sure it's being run to my liking, but now that I have Jay, maybe I could set aside some time.

Dragging my hands across my face, trying to wake up, I will myself to head out to the bar. Before I leave, I take in the sight of my small office. Feelings of being blessed rush to the front of my mind. The wooden desk sitting in front of me isn't anything special. It's large, old, and covered with scratches, but it's suitable for what I need. Sitting across from the desk are two old wood chairs being held together by a splinter. A tall metal filing cabinet stands in the corner and across from it, on the other side of the room, sits a large worn-out black leather sofa.

The only new thing in my office are the walls that are covered with a fresh coat of cream paint. Pride surges through me. Except for my office, I have updated all the furnishings in what used to be an old rundown bar I bought a year ago. Friends gifted me their old furniture that I've filled my office with, and saving everywhere I can have helped me with cost because currently I'm turning the large space upstairs into an apartment.

If these walls could talk, I know the stories they would tell could make even the best of whores blush. This old biker bar used to be known for the flock of rowdy crowds having open sex and taking part in drugs. It would be nothing surprising to see on any night. My lips curve upward, thinking of old man Griff and how he and his wife ran this place. Only when his beloved wife passed did he decide close it. He mentioned he didn't want to run it since it was her dream and being without her hurt too much, coming to opening it up every day.

Griff wouldn't sell this place to just anyone. He made damn sure I proved myself to him. I worked on his farm for six months. Shoveling shit wasn't my finest moment, but I was determined to win over his approval. After putting me through the test of sleeping on a cot in his barn and making me shovel shit out of his cow pasture along with the horse stalls, he finally said I had learned what hard work and determination were. He told me I would need that drive when hard times would hit, and I needed to do what it took to keep this place open.

I look at my clock on the wall. Shit, it's closing time. I slept longer than I should have. I did not intend to drift off, but sleep took over. When I stand up, my hand brushes my pants. I curse myself without having to look down. I already know what it's from. Shaking my head at myself for the uncontrollable wet dreams I've been having of being buried between Maggie's legs, I head upstairs to change.

When I get to the top of the stairs, I swing the door open to my apartment. It's not much right now. The walls are still bare from the lack of sheetrock. The electric and plumbing are currently under construction. I requested the guest bathroom be finished first and lucky for me, Shadow finished it today. He worked on it during the day since the bar doesn't open till five in the evening. The man is from another breed. He could easily pass for a grizzly bear with his size.

When I make it to the bathroom, I slide my jeans and briefs off and throw them to the side. They land crotch up, staring at me in the face as if they're laughing at my expense.

Fucking wet dreams!

It's been close to three months since I've seen Maggie's gorgeous face. Three long fucking months. I've searched any social media accounts, camped out at what I thought was her apartment complex. It was the apartment complex where she ran straight into my chest. I've had women run into me on purpose, but they did nothing to make my body burn the way she does. Beautiful, sassy, headstrong, and a rack that I could bury my cock in.

I had stayed with a friend for a few months before I decided to build an apartment above my bar. Sometimes the clubhouse can be too much, and I need a place to crash from the noise after a long day.

Washing myself up, I pull a pair of jeans out of a hamper. Deciding to go commando, I slide them on and head down to the bar.

I walk in just in time to see Jay closing the double doors behind the last customer. Jay is my right-hand man, and a damn good manager. I was right to hire him. His size and manners scare the hell out of people. We've never had a problem with anyone causing trouble, but I'm not willing to risk all the hard work I've put into this place for it to get wrecked to hell and back.

One of my bartenders, Nina, is pulling out the money tray from the register to count it.

"I can count the register tonight," I announce.

Nina is around my age—twenty two—long black hair, big blue eyes and covered in ink. The one and most important drawback is that she's lazier than a turd sunbathing on a sidewalk.

"Okay, boss. Mind if I head out?"

"Nina, we need to talk." I tilt my head to the barstool in front of me.

I haven't been looking forward to this. Letting employees go is something I dislike, but as the owner, sometimes it's necessary when they're not performing. Since the rest of the team is in the kitchen cleaning up, I figure this is as good a time as ever to have that talk.

She pulls out the barstool, taking a seat without a trace of concern etched on her face.

Jay remains standing at the front door, waiting for what is coming. He's been informing me she's been standing around talking to guys and snacking on the food without paying for it. My other employees work hard, and they don't deserve to have to do her job too.

Inhaling, I begin, "Nina, we've had discussions in the past about your actions. You're not helping the others and you continue to eat and not pay for it." Pausing my words, I give her a moment to let it soak in that she's about to get fired. I continue. "I've put you on notice, but this time I'm going to have to let you go."

Her face contorts into anger, and I prepare myself to get a tongue lashing because Nina is anything but graceful enough to bow out peacefully. Instead of a tongue lashing, she picks up a half filled glass with liquor and pulls her arm back and slings it forward. I try to jump to grab her arm, but I slip on the contents when she throws the glass and I fall, but not before the glass hits my collarbone, making me curl my shoulders, hitting the bar as I fall down. I scream out in pain. Doing my best to suck it up, I jump to my feet, stumbling backward to rest my ass against the countertop. Jay has already made his way over to her side, ready to show her ass to the door. Before he throws her out, she gives me a mouth full of words that I'm pretty sure Webster doesn't even know, then she throws me a farewell by raising her middle finger. Once Jay locks the door behind her, he comes back over to me.

"That went well," he chuckles.

I turn around and pain shoots through my shoulder, making me double over in pain.

"Fuck man. You, okay?"

"My shoulder hurts like a bitch." My face scrunches up. "I think that bitch may have broken my collarbone.

Jay comes over closer, inspecting it. "Yeah, it looks to be broken. I'm calling Shadow to bring his truck. I rode my bike tonight."

When we finally hear Shadow pull up outside, we walk out to meet him and Jay locks the door behind us. When I climb in, Jay stands at the door, trying to start some shit.

"Fucking hell man, glad you could make it." Jay yells.

"I've been busy." Shadow retorts in his deep voice. I notice his knuckles are freshly cut and covered in blood stains.

Instead of asking questions, I yell out to Jay, "Get in the fucking truck!" I'm not in a mood for banter. Just get my ass to the hospital.

Shadow pulls out of the parking lot, stomping on the gas, making us shift in our seats.

"Fucking hell, man. You could take it a little easier?"

Twenty minutes later, we're pulling up to the entrance to the local emergency room.

"I'm going to park the truck," Shadow says after I crawl out.

Walking into the lobby, I make my way up to an older lady sitting at the front desk. When Jay and I approach, her eyes go wide. I imagine with two men over six feet and enormous statures, and the fact Jay is wearing his cut would seem scary to anyone. Her hand moves under the desk, and it doesn't take a rocket scientist to know she has a panic button under there.

"Gentlemen, can I help you?" her voice comes out shaky.

"I need to see a doctor." I bellow out, hoping she gets the hint to hurry the fuck up. When she doesn't respond, I tell her, "My collarbone is broken."

She rustles around with bullshit paper and hands them off to me.

"Name?" She types it on her computer as I give it to her. "When you complete those forms, bring them back to me. I've got you checked in. If they call you before you finish, you can take them to the back with you and the nurse will retrieve them from you."

"I'm not able to fill anything out. It's my good arm that has something wrong with it. Can I just tell you my information?"

She gives me a scowl.

"Can you fill out these forms, or do you have something wrong with your arm?" She asks Jay in a sour tone.

"Yeah." He takes the forms from her, and we take a seat in the waiting room.

Fifteen minutes later, we get called to the back. A brunette woman with shoulder length hair and round brown eyes walks in. She's tiny, only around five-three.

"Hello, my name is Jenevein and I'll be your nurse. Do you have paperwork?"

Handing them to her, she breezes through them, asking additional questions, then starts poking at me. Pain shoots through my shoulder, making me grit my teeth, praying she'll hurry.

Give me some pain medicine, all ready.

"Well, I think it's definitely broken. How did you break it?" the nurse asks.

Doing my best to avoid her question, I ask her, "How long will this take?" I don't rat. In my world, we don't sell out others. If there is anything that needs to be dealt with, I'll take care of it.

"When we get your scans, then we'll be able to tell you more. You," she says to Jay, "We're going to be taking him for a CT scan. Are you related?"

Jay smiles a huge pearly white smile. "He's my brother."

He's not wrong. We are brothers, but not by blood, by choice.

The nurse tucks her face into her neck, blushing. Clearing her throat, she fixes her composure. She turns to lay her tablet down on my bed and Jay steps closer to her. When she turns, she bumps into him.

"Sorry," she whispers.

Jay grins at her with his hand on his dick, adjusting himself.

Fucking hell!

She side-steps him and opens the double glass doors to the room. Coming back to the bed, she unlocks the wheels and starts pushing the bed out. "He'll be back in a bit if you want to sit in here and wait. There are also vending machines down the hall to the right."

"I'll be here." He grins.

Once I've had a scan, and they wheel me back to the room, the pain has slacked off.

"Just try to relax. I gave you some pain medicine in your IV, so hopefully that will kick in."

I want to tell her it has, but when I open my mouth, the words don't escape because at that moment Shadow grabs my attention. The nurse's eyes go wide when his frame takes up the doorway. Her hands begin to shake as she clumsily hooks me back to the monitor and dots out of the room, leaving a horny

Jay standing with his mouth open and dick hard.

Shaking the nasty thoughts out of his head, he throws Shadow a dirty look. "Where the hell have you been?"

As usual, Shadow shrugs and gives no excuse. The man is a complete vault. No one is ever going to get him to open up enough to get the slightest information. There's no doubt we can always rely on him never to spill any club secrets.

When the doctor walks in, Shadow stands straighter, leaning against the wall. His cold eyes never leave her. I have to admit, she's beautiful. Blonde streaks of hair pulled up in a bun with skin so smooth and no blemishes. She looks too much like a porcelain doll. Her white coat is hanging loosely around her, but when she moves and the coat flares open, you can see hints of a curvy body.

"Well, Mr.—"

"Colt."

"Okay. Mr. Colt," she says, all business. "Your collarbone is indeed broken. There's not much we can do. We'll put your arm in a sling, and it'll take six to eight weeks to heal. You will need to call your physician to make a follow-up appointment."

I hear nothing after the comment she makes on how many weeks my collarbone will heal. All I can think of is that I can forget about riding my bike anytime soon. Plus, I will need to hire additional help at the bar. My mind is going into overdrive mode on making a mental checklist for things to accomplish.

Hiring someone for the office is also a top priority. Fuck! I'm disgusted with myself for letting this happen, but hell, what's worst is not being able to ride my bike. It's going to suck balls.

Once I'm released, the doctor insists that I leave the hospital in a wheelchair. Complying with her orders, I give in, and Shadow and Jay go get the truck to bring it around.

The nurse wheels me out and when we get into the lobby, that's when I hear a voice that I only hear in my dreams. That beautiful sassy voice wraps around my mind, whispering she's mine.

Frantically looking all around me, I see her. It's Maggie. She's in the elevator with some pencil looking dick dressed in a business suit.

Trying to climb my way out of the wheelchair, my feet get tangled and I take a slow fall, not taking my eyes off her. I turn my body, trying not to land on my right side. Maggie doesn't notice me, even with all the commotion I'm causing.

I bang my fist on the concrete floor. "Fuckkk!"

Just my luck. She looked so damn beautiful in her skirt that showed her sexy legs and that white blouse that was so thin I could see the lacy camisole she had on underneath.

"Fuck man," Jay says when he enters back into the lobby, rushing to me. "What the hell are you doing?"

I can't even answer. All I can think about is seeing Maggie with some guy when it should have been me and what was she doing here?

***

It's been a long week. Flashes of Maggie have invaded my mind while leaving me with an uneasy feeling that she's moved on. Maybe with that skinny dick I saw her with. On top of that, I still haven't hired anyone to replace Nina. The only good thing that came about this week was I have temporary help in the office—Susan is the wife of one of my brothers from Fallen Saints MC Club.

She's been an enormous help this week, recording all the receipts and making sure all the books are in top shape. The only problem is she's not interested in working full time, because she's a stay home mom. Thankfully, she said she would stay on till I find someone full time, or for however long her mother could keep the kids.

I'm wiping down the bar when Jay parks his ass on a barstool with a look that is a bit more serious than what he usually sports.

"Something wrong?" I ask.

He gives me a hard look and I have a feeling this is more about me than him.

"What's going on with you? J-Bird called me. He's concerned about you. We've all noticed a difference in you since you came back from your dad's lake house. Do we need to put a hit out on someone?"

His voice may sound a little lighter at the end of that sentence, but I can see in his eyes that a hit would be made if I was to say the word. Pride surges through me, knowing my brothers will always have

28

my back. The thought of telling him about Maggie passes briefly through my mind, but I dismiss it. I don't need anyone knowing about Maggie, not right now, maybe ever. Her body, face, and mind belong to me, no one else. I'm not wanting to share anything about her, not yet.

"My brother—Joel is getting married next weekend. You should come with me. There's always women at weddings ready to get laid," He grins wickedly. "Something about a wedding makes them horny," he wiggles his eyebrows.

I laugh at him because the man is always thinking about getting laid. Maybe I should go. I know Joel from hanging out with Jay. It's not like I would be crashing his wedding.

"Yeah, count me in. Do I need to get a present? Don't people usually take a gift to those things?"

Jay stands up, "Up to you. I'm giving them the gift of my presence."

CHAPTER 3

Maggie

For Heaven's sake. This guy will not shut up. I glance at my watch, wishing this date was over. Hart, my date, works at the car dealership where I just finished up doing some consulting work. I dodged him on every attempt he made to ask me out, giving him the excuse that I had a strict policy of no dating employees where I worked but on my last day, he basically cornered me, mentioning that since I wouldn't be working there any longer there shouldn't be a conflict. He wasn't supposed to know it was my last day, because it was supposed to be between the manager and his secretary, but I have a feeling that big nosey Marie ran her mouth.

At the mere mention of my last day, I wanted to rip off her head for giving him the message.

So here I am, doing my best to pay this douche bag attention because he clearly needs it. He has told me all about his job and how great he is at it and if I had a gun, I would either shoot him or myself just for this to be over.

"Having the highest sales for the past five years makes me the top earning employee for the company. I can't even tell you how important…"

Blah blah blah. Just shut up already. Easing my phone out of my purse, I send out a S.O.S text to Macy. Her text comes back immediately, saying she's calling now. Quickly throwing my phone back into my bag to make sure he suspects nothing. It rings as soon as it lands.

Holding up a finger, I say, "Oh hold that sentence, I need to get this," I try to sound as if I've been paying attention to his self-stroking ego and that I'm truly interested in what he was saying, when it's the farthest from the truth.

"Hello," I act surprise that I'm getting interrupted.

Macy's voice comes through in a whisper. "Going that bad?"

"Yes. It is?" I raise an eyebrow dramatically.

"Oh, you're good," Macy giggles, letting me know she finds this too damn funny.

"Yes. Okay, I'm on my way." I click end and reach for my purse as I slide out of the booth. The jerk drives a Beemer but asked me out to a fast-food restaurant, ordering us hamburgers and french fries, then slides a coupon across the counter. I mean, who does that on a first date? A cheap ass, that's who.

"I have to go. That was my sister. She's sick," I tell

him while trying to imitate a pained expression of having to leave.

"I can drive you," he says as he tries to slide out of the booth.

I reach out, touching his hand, "No, she doesn't really feel like having company but me. She's been going through a lot lately and she just needs her sis."

He lights up to my touch. "I'll call you. Give me your number."

"No," I say a little too quick. "I'll call you. Just write your number down for me." I hand him my napkin and grab a pen out of my bag.

He scribbles it down and passes it back.

"Don't get up, please stay and enjoy your meal." before he has a chance to say anything, I all but run out of the hamburger joint, hoping I never have to see him again.

When I get into my car, I dial Macy and make plans with her for the next day to go over the last of the wedding details. Her wedding is this weekend. Thank goodness I've had her wedding to distract me from the war inside my head.

Pressing the gas pedal, I pick up speed in desperate need to make it home to relieve some of this tension built up. A warm bath and a cold press to my forehead with a glass of wine in one hand sounds like a glorious end to a terrible night.

***

The next day, Macy and I are sitting on her couch when Joel, her fiancé, walks in. His eyes rest on Macy,

32

love and heat swirling in them. It's the perfect combination. I can't help but envy their relationship. Exhaling, I try to look away when he presses his lips to hers, greeting her with a kiss.

My phone vibrates on the coffee table, and I can see it's another text from Charles. I've told him to move on because I have, even if it's a lie, but he doesn't seem to care. It's funny. He didn't put this much effort into calling or messaging me when he had me. Instead, he cheated on me with his childhood first love. I can't say I'm any better than him, because I allowed Colt to touch me in places I shouldn't have, but after Charles treated me like nothing for months, it had me wanting to feel wanted by someone. Colt just happened to be his step-brother who was stupidly hot, and could have been a heart surgeon with the way he worked his hands. I swipe the screen to clear the message.

"Was that Charles again?" Macy asks.

"Yes, he seems to think he's still invited to the wedding. We broke up almost three months ago. What part doesn't he understand?"

"Have you told him he doesn't get a second chance? Sometimes people don't get the message till you spell it out for them," Macy tells me.

"Well, let's see," I put my finger on my chin. "He was the first one to say he wanted to break up with me because we were...different. Basically, he thought he was better than me," I widen my eyes. "Can you believe that?" I huff. "Then when little Ms. Sunshine only bought a ticket for a one time ride on the small pecker express, he comes crawling back to me. So, the way I look at it, he doesn't deserve any explanation other than no Charles, it's not happening again." I slouch against the couch.

"My brother is going to be at the wedding!" Joel informs me with a wide grin.

"Joel, you forget, I'm very well aware of your brother's reputation. Macy has already tried to play matchmaker. Thank you, but no thank you. I'm ready for something… you know… like you guys have. I'm tired of being the one in the relationship who's making… sacrifices," my voice trails off. Tears build up and I need them to stop. I don't want to cry, and I don't need my best friend to feel bad about what she has.

Macy moves out of Joel's embrace. Reaching over to me, she wraps her arms around me. "You're going to find it. Don't give up."

Swiping the tears that were determined to fall, I plastered a smile on my face. "Let's not talk about me. This is your week. Let's finish these table settings."

"I'll go make some coffee. Are you girls going to go at it all night?" Joel asks.

"No coffee for me," Macy and I say at the same time.

"I have another client tomorrow morning," I inform them. "I need to leave soon."

Since being dumped by Charles, I decided I wanted to make a change. I quit my job and became a consultant for companies that need help keeping better records of their books. Thank goodness I had a good savings account built up, because at first it was really slow, but it's been picking up since I did my first job. They were a large family chain restaurant and the word of my work spread fast though them.

"You didn't tell me you had another job so soon," Macy says with excitement.

"Yeah, things are really taking off," I smile. It feels good to experience something going right for a change, at last.

We finish up the table decorations just before ten. After helping clean up, I hug Macy and Joel goodnight.

I need to head home to prepare for my meeting tomorrow. Then I plan on relaxing in a tub of hot water before I jump in the bed.

The next morning, I put on my usual business attire; a black pencil skirt and a midnight blue blouse that makes my eyes pop. Stepping into my pumps, I head out. I'm meeting the new client at his place of business. It's a small family restaurant on the outskirts of the city.

Thirty minutes into the drive, and the traffic comes to a crawl. Shit! I'm going to be late. Shooting a text to the owner, I let him know I'm stuck in traffic. A deep loud vibrating rumble surrounds me, making my car hum to the loud pipes on a bike. A man dressed in a helmet and sunglasses with a short sleeve white shirt and jeans creeps up between cars. When the man on the bike comes next to my car, I look out my window just as he hits my side-view mirror.

"Son of a bitch!" I yell out to no one.

Either he didn't notice that he just hit my car or didn't care. Regardless, my blood rises. He could have waited like the rest of us. Turning my blinker on to exchange lanes, I move over to the faster lane, determined to catch up with the biker. Finally, we move past the wreck that's been holding traffic up and I speed up to the motorcycle where the hulk of a beast looks to be having a joyful ride without caring that he just messed up my mirror.

I pull up to the side of his motorcycle, honking and pointing at my mirror.

"Yeah, asshole, you messed up my mirror," again I'm yelling to myself because I know he can't hear me.

He smiles and I almost lose control of my car. Fuck, he's hot! Calm down Maggie. He's trying to distract you with all those perfect white straight teeth and that smile that I'm sure gets women in his bed.

The guy glides his motorcycle over to my driver's side with an effortless motion and I point to my mirror, showing him what he did. Then I reach out my window and give it a tug, afraid it might fall off. Humiliation settles over me when my mirror pops back into place.

Smooth Maggie, just smooth.

I feel like a complete dumbass. Tucking my head in my shoulders, I wave at the biker, trying my best to speed up. He holds to my speed, and I take a chance and glance over to him. He smiles, extends his arm with his cell phone in his hand and a number on the screen. It has to be his number. I contemplate on calling him immediately because I could use a good rumble between the sheets, but who am I kidding? I'm not that type of girl. Relationships are usually my MO. One-night stands are not my thing. Then I think about Colt and how I let him… I squeeze my eyes shut, feeling the burn of my embarrassment spread from my neck to my cheeks. I'm such a slut!

I take the next exit off the interstate, waving to him before he races past me. His black vest has his club on the back, Fallen Saints MC. It's the same club Joel's brother is in. I bet that man could be all kinds of trouble. The kind that would leave you to wanting more. Thank goodness I didn't pick up my phone to call him. I'd be hot, wet, and left alone again when he got his fill.

CHAPTER 4

Colt

The amount of customers tonight is overwhelming. Friday nights are usually busy, but fuck me, tonight is crazy. With the use of my one arm, I attempt to do my best in assisting behind the bar, and later in helping clear away tables.

Two staff members called in sick and we're short a bartender since I cut Nina loose. The newbie working behind the bar is barely twenty-one and is slow as hell. I can't blame him. He was supposed to be fully trained by Nina. She only did half a job with not only her duties but also training the newbie, and now I've had to throw him in full bartender mode. He's just got to learn as we go.

Empty glasses and beer bottles are piling up on the tables and I'm playing bus boy along with bartender tonight. Frustrated and annoyed, I let my anger get the best of me when I drop a tumbler into the bucket with a little more force than I should. The glass shatters when it lands with a thump. I shake my head. What a fucking nightmare tonight has turned out to be!

Hands slide around my waist, pressing their large breasts against my back. I look up at the ceiling, closing my eyes. I already know by her touch it's Sabrina.

Sabrina, who used to be a causal hookup, didn't get the message when I told her it was over. She's a cool chick that you can have a good time with, but now the thought of someone else touching me does nothing for me. I only want one set of hands to caress my body.

"Colt," she says with a purr that does nothing for me. Her claws scrape my shirt as they slide up my torso. "I miss you," she drags the word 'you' out.

I turn around, hoping to step aside to put distance between us, only to fail when Sabrina steps closer. "Sabrina, I'm trying to work," I reply firmly, placing my hands on her shoulders.

She blinks, looking up at me, stunned I've turned her down again. Used to be, I would grab her up and haul her to my office, pushing her onto her knees, but Maggie's put some kind of black magic on my dick, and it doesn't rise to the thought of anyone but her.

Her fingers circle my chest. "Colt, you haven't touched me in months. Why? I know you want me."

"Don't make a scene. We've been over this. It was fun until it wasn't. We're done." I've done my best to be nice, and tried to tell her I wasn't interested anymore. But she keeps holding on, thinking I will change my mind.

"I'll wait. You just need… time to realize I'm made for you."

I inhale, because some women are a stage five on clinginess. Those types I can usually spot right off because they are way over eager to do whatever I ask. I didn't see any of those signs in Sabrina. Now I wonder if she was hiding it really well.

"Let me spell it out for you, IT'S. NOT. GOING. TO HAPPEN. Not today, not tomorrow, never."

Her face contorts into anger, but she quickly recovers and pretends to cry. No tears. Her body doesn't quiver, only her bottom lip pokes out like a fucking child.

"Colt," Katie calls me from the bar, waving me over.

"I have to go." I walk away feeling like an ass, not for ending it, but for raising my voice at her. If she hadn't gone stage five clinger on me, I wouldn't have felt the need to do what I did.

My mother would have been really disappointed in me if she had heard me talk to a woman like that, but then again, my mother would have never approved of someone like Sabrina. She died when I was nine. An aneurysm took her from me. I've learned to deal with the pain of losing her, but I still have days that hurt more than others.

After mom died, Connie—my stepmother, came

into the picture and her pussy of a son Charles. Charles is harmless, but has always been a thorn in my side. He's like the bitchy sisters Cinderella had. Jealously radiates off him in gigantic waves. Anything I had, he had to have. He would have a fit if he didn't get whatever I had.

"Taste this." Katie holds up a spoon of what could be a soup.

I let her slip it into my mouth and I close my eyes. "Shit, Katie. That's good!"

She smiles, "Thank you. I made it for tomorrow's special. I thought maybe you would think about opening up for lunch. It would bring more business in and we could put together a small menu for lunch."

I've been giving some thought to opening for lunch, but until now I haven't had a cook worth a shit to do that. Now I have the dilemma of being short staffed. If we are going to open up for lunch, I have to have office help along with extra staff.

Jay jumps in front of me, taking the spoon from Katie, "Give me a bite," he dips the spoon back into the bowl and inhales it, "Fuck, Katie. That shit is good. What is it?"

"It's toad intestines stew," she says with a serious face.

Jay turns green and darts to the back.

Katie and I bust out laughing.

"Seriously, what's in that?" I ask curiously. Please don't say toad intestines.

"Steak stew," she yells over her shoulder as she

walks back into the kitchen.

Later that night, Jay strolls into my office. Grabbing the seat across from me, he props his feet up on my desk.

"Aren't you supposed to be working?" I raise an eyebrow at him.

"Break time. You still coming tomorrow?" He asks.

"Yep, I'll be there. You said it's at the Hallmark house, right?"

"Too bad you can't ride your bike. The weather is going to be perfect on Saturday."

I nod without looking up. I'm too evolved in why my inventory is not matching up with the cash flow. Getting annoyed with the computer, I slam the buttons when I press them.

"Fuck," I say as I punch enter.

"Do I need to go get Sabrina to come in here and suck you off to happy land?"

Hell no!

"I can't get this shit to balance."

"Macy has a friend that could help. Joel's been trying to play fix up. He says she is smart." He grimaces. "You know what that means? She got hit with the fucking ugly stick."

"What if she's hot?"

"Well, a nice set of tits to suck on always puts me in a good mood. I'll soon find out."

"Get your ass back to work. Your break is over." I reach over and shove his feet off my desk.

Standing up, he walks to my door and turns to

face me. "I'm getting you laid this weekend, and that's a promise. I can't take your grumpy ass anymore," he walks out, but not before he throws a balled up paper at me, hitting me on the forehead. "See you tomorrow," he says a little too cheerfully.

Shithead. Wait, did he say he'd see me tomorrow? "Jay," I yell out, panicking.

He pops his head back into my office. "You forgot. I've got to do the best man thing tonight. Something about rehearsal. If you ask me, it's just walking someone down the aisle. Big deal."

Fuck! I forgot.

With a heavy breath, I shut my computer down and follow him out to where Cody is working his ass off behind the bar, taking orders and mixing drinks.

CHAPTER 5

Maggie

I'm dragging my feet as we walk from the pillar that Macy and Joel will exchange their vows under to the large tent where the rehearsal dinner is being held. I can't shake this sheet of patheticness that has consumed me tonight. This is supposed to be a joyous occasion, so why do I feel like shit?

At the entryway I spot the bar and my eyes zoom in on what I want. Wine. Making a beeline for it, I head straight to the young man that's mixing drinks.

"White Zinfandel please. Fill it to the brim," I command in a rush.

When I bring the glass to my lips, I close my eyes and take a mouthful.

So good!

I watch everyone offering their blessings to the soon to be married couple, then I focus on the lavish decorations that Macy and I worked so hard on. The beautiful floral centerpieces decorated in fall colors of purple and yellow give off a radiant, rich vibe. Taller vases with floating candles are lined up with the floral arrangements. It's breathtaking to see everything put in place for the event.

When I raise my cup again to take another gulp, I realize it's empty. Shit. I really want another glass, but since I'm a light drinker, I think better of it. I won't be able to give my speech without slurring my words if I have too much. My nerves get the better of me when I think about tomorrow's speech in front of three hundred guests. Maybe I could just grab half a glass.

I'm about to walk back to the bar when Joel's brother, Jay, strolls up with a very smug grin. He's very attractive with his enormous size and good looks. He's got the whole biker thing locked down, dressed in black boots, ripped blue jeans and a black t-shirt that looks like it could fit my twenty-pound poodle.

"So you're Macy's bestie?" He looks me up and down.

My ovaries stay in place, not swooning. I blame it on the fact that he's slept with half the city. I don't know him personally, but I know men like him and I want nothing to do with their type.

"Yes. You're Joel's brother, right?" He gives me a smug grin.

Cocky much?

"You've heard of me?" His eyes light up like he's

the best thing since ice cream.

"Well, to be fair," I think fast on my feet. "Your name came up at work. You know the health department?"

He throws his head back with a deep laugh, bringing his eyes back to me. He says, "I like a challenge."

Well, shit! That didn't go as I expected.

Someone taps their glass, calling for us to have a seat.

Jay walks along beside me and when we get to the table, he pulls out my seat. I'm a bit taken aback because I never expected him to be a gentleman, but I shouldn't be surprised. I know Mrs. Mitchell, Joel and Jay's mom, expects her boys to have manners. I've seen what she can do with a fly swatter and it's not a pretty sight to see a grown man to cower, namely Joel. When I take the seat, my eyes find her. She's eyeing Jay, giving him a nod like she's saying good boy.

"Would you like a refill?" Jay asks.

I shake my head and he takes the seat beside me, putting his arm around the back of my seat. Joel and Macy are sitting at their own table in front of us, and I can see a scheme building up in their eyes.

Would I want someone like Jay?

I question myself, wondering if I was too judgemental about Jay's dating history. Everyone has a history. His is just... a little more than most. Maybe that's something I need, just a one-night stand of boundless sex. I doubt a man like Jay would let his woman go unsatisfied, unlike Charles.

Looking down at his thick thighs, I remember who else had thick, strong thighs. Colt. I squeeze my legs together, trying to release the built up frustration that I've been feeling for months. Ever since I left his dad's lake house. The mere thought of Colt has my core aching for his fingers, except I want more than his fingers. I want all of him.

Move on Maggie. You're never going to see him again.

Fingers linger over my exposed shoulder as Jay leans into my ear, "Being this close to me having an effect on you, Baby Girl?"

I roll my eyes. Seriously. I whisper back, "Jay, the only effect you're giving me is creepy vibes," he chuckles.

Leaning more into me, his voice is low, "I love it when a woman's role play is denial. It lets me show them what a real man like me can do."

Well, holy fuck!

***

"Macy," tears spring to my eyes as my best friend looks at herself in the mirror, "You look… beautiful!" Her dress fits her perfectly. It's a gorgeous white ball gown with a princess V-neck court train lace satin dress that looks like it was custom made to hug her figure.

She smiles to fight the tears, but the redness in her eyes gives her away. I take a tissue from the makeup artist table and hand to her, "Here, don't mess up your makeup just yet," I wink, trying to bring a little humor into the moment.

She blots her eyes, trying hard not to mess up the work of the makeup artist.

"I just can't believe this day is here," she says, trying to hold her sobs.

"There's no one that deserves it more than you, Macy," I tell her honestly. She's had her share of toads, but Joel is definitely a keeper.

"I have a feeling your day is coming, and who knows? We might be sisters-in-law," she giggles.

"It's just a date. Let's not get ahead of ourselves," I tell Macy, knowing that Jay would be someone I only see myself with for a good time.

After being worn down, I finally agreed to one date with Jay. He's right, he really enjoys a challenge. The way he wouldn't ease off after I kept pouring out excuses last night after dinner wore me out. So finally, I agreed.

"Here, don't forget your bouquet," she looks at it and the charm that is dangling from a ribbon. It's a picture of her grandparents that she was so close to. "You know —"

"Time to roll, ladies," the wedding planner yells from the other side of the door.

"Ready?" I ask, inhaling, trying to calm my own nerves.

CHAPTER 6

Colt

The sounds of chatter are loud when I get out of my truck in front of the Hallmark House.

The house has been a symbol in the community for as long as I've been alive. It sits back a mile from the road, lined with majestic oak trees on each side of the driveway, like soldiers of the past greeting you as you move by.

I follow the path of voices until I reach the area where the ceremony will be held. All the chairs face an arch where flowers are intertwined into it making the setting feel whimsical.

Jay spots me, giving me a head tilt. He says something to his brother and heads my way.

"Didn't think you were going to show," he pulls me in for a brotherly hug. "There are some hot chicks here. I'll introduce you when this shindig is over," he wiggles his eyebrows. "I'm committed."

"Committed?" I ask, confused.

"Yeah, to getting you laid," he laughs.

Only if you knew, brother. Only if you knew.

"I'm telling you weddings are where it's at to meet women. Guess who has a date with the maid of honor? That's right, yours truly," he pretends to straighter his cuffs, like he's James Bond.

I laugh this time because Jay works it, no matter where we go or where we are. He's always charming the women.

My cell vibrates, and I slide it out, hoping Kaitlyn —a new manager I hired—doesn't need me. I panic a little when I see it's from my dad. He rarely calls unless he's trying to get me to come over for a holiday. He knows I'm way too busy and extra time isn't something I have right now.

"I've got to grab this. See you after the ceremony," Jay nods and heads back to his brother. "Wait, where do I put this gift?" He points over to a table where there're boxes with bows stack on top of one another.

Quickly swiping my phone, I bring it up to my ear, "Dad, something wrong?"

"Nothing, I just wanted to call and say hey to my boy," he says, sounding tired.

My dad is a good man. He treats my step-mother better than she should be treated. When my mother passed, I could tell he was lost. I didn't fuss or complain when he married Connie. I knew he was trying his best to live without my mother.

"Dad," a familiar song plays behind me. The one

letting you know it's time for the couple to say I do. "I'm at a wedding. Can I call you back?"

"Go on. I'll catch up with you later." he hangs up and an uneasy feeling starts in the pit of my stomach.

When I take a seat, I can see all the bridesmaids are lined up and when I see Jay standing with the woman I've been dreaming of, beating myself off to, I think I must have died.

Fuck yeah!

My eyes wander down her body, soaking in her beauty. The deep purple dress that showcases her legs makes me groan, and my hand itches to be between them again. To feel how tight her muscles are and how she squeezes my fingers when she comes. Fuck!

I grip the chair because I want to rip my friend's arm off for touching her when her arm interlocks with his.

Maggie's eyes look straight ahead, and I can tell she's nervous about the sizeable crowd with all their eyes on her. I inhale and then exhale, trying to keep calm when Jay leans too close to her, whispering in her ear. Then realization dawns on me, and I want to scream. This cannot be happening! She can't be the woman Jay has a fucking date with. She's mine!

My fucking jaw hurts from me clenching it during the ceremony. After the couple said I do, they moved us to a large tent where a bar, a dance floor, and waiters are walking around offering appetizers.

"Jack and coke," I growl at the bartender.

It's not his fault I'm in a shit mood, but I can't help

but to bark at him. I can't help but to pace, eagerly waiting on the wedding party to get done with pictures I take this time to soak in as much alcohol as I can.

Fucking hell, how long does it take?

When I've consumed just enough alcohol, the wedding party comes into the tent and I spot Jay with his arm around Maggie. My grip tightens on my drink as I crush it, warm liquid spilling over my hand.

"Fuck," I whisper under my breath.

Holding the drink away from me so the rest doesn't spill on my clothes, I walk back to the bar to grab a handful of napkins and wipe myself off. Solely focus on wiping off the wasted acholic, I hear a nagging voice that I've known since childhood.

Fucking Charles!

The wedding party made their way to the front, and that's where I see Charles. His hair is longer than normal, and he's completely disarrayed. His clothes look filthy and old. I move in a little closer, but not close enough for Maggie to notice me.

Observing the commotion Charles is causing, I stand off to the side. He's groveling to Maggie, and I can see the distress in her eyes. I take a step forward to pull him away, but I stop when Jay intervenes, standing like a giant over Charles. Picking Charles up like a rag doll, he heads out of the tent with him. Only Charles' ratty shirt tears, ripping apart in Jay's hand, Charles falls flat on his ass. A chuckle escapes my lips. This is really comical to watch. Of all people, I would have never guessed Charles would fall from grace like a burning building collapsing.

CHAPTER 7

Maggie

Charles' showing up has shaken me. I nervously fumble with my dress, trying to hide the embarrassment that's bubbling inside me. I never would have thought Charles would do something so desperate. After he claimed we were too different and I was beneath him, I would have thought he would have moved on. He and Nat seem perfect for one another. They were both on the same level. The level where you're in between childhood and adulthood. You still think of only yourself before others. Yeah, that one.

Jay more than handled the problem and for that, I'm relieved. I'm not sure if he could see how upset I was or if it was a chance for him to get his hands dirty with blood. Something tells me he enjoys intimidating others along with beating the crap out of them.

Speaking of the devil himself, he struts back into

the tent with a smile that I could only describe as amusement. I'm sure his size makes him feel like King Kong. He's standing around six-one, but his muscles are larger than most of the men I've ever seen. Other than one other man. I've had the pleasure of being pressed up against.

"Are you okay?" Jay asks.

I nod, but I know I'm not. I don't know how to feel.

The D.J. taps on the microphone getting everyone's attention, "I want to introduce to you Mr. and Mrs. Joel Huntingburg!"

The music cranks up as Macy and Joel walk in holding hands and dancing onto the dance floor. Everyone claps and it seems the outburst is forgotten as the evening kicks in.

After the newlywed couple cuts the cake, everyone takes their seat and I know it's my time to make my speech. Tapping my glass, I stand up, "I want to make a toast," holding up my glass I continue. "To the new couple. May your marriage be filled with happiness, and your hearts filled with love, and Macy, may you never have to call Bob again to do Joel's handy work," I wink at Macy and she laughs with a few others knowing exactly what the hell I'm referring to.

Everyone cheers, "Here, here."

A few hours later, when the non-partiers go home, the lights go dim and the atmosphere changes to more of a club style vibe. When couples make their way to the dance floor, I stay planted in my chair, not bothering to look up. Concentrating on the napkin in my hands, I twist and pick it apart. I should get up and socialize with the other bridesmaids who have all gathered at the edge of the dance floor, talking in a deep conversation, but I don't have it in me. My body is tired from these past two weeks of running around gathering and collecting items for this beautiful event.

When April, the girl I can't stand, turns to her left and smiles at someone, I crane my neck to see who's got her attention. I jump when someone's breath fans my skin.

"I need a dance," the deep voice says. "You owe me a date."

Jay.

My cheeks heat with discomfort. I really don't know why I agreed to go out with him. His good looks and bad boy persona make me want to run away. I can't visualize him as being husband material. A good fuck, of course. He's everything you would want sweating over you, but I'm not looking for a good fuck, so why did I agree?

Sliding my chair back, I stand, only to face Jay as he softly wraps his hand around my waist, pulling me out of the dance floor. The music changes to a slower beat and I place my hands on his shoulders.

I'm about to step into his embrace when my body is jerked backwards. I gasp when I stumble up against something solid. My body instantly melts. There's one person who my body has ever melted for, Colt.

"Your body remembers me, hmm?" He brushes his lips against my ear. "Does your pussy remember my fingers, or should I reintroduce them?"

Words catch in my throat as his cologne attacks my body in ways that should be illegal. I've only been this close to him in my dreams and it's nowhere near as invigorating as the real live version. His body was molded in the image of the gods.

Jay steps closer with confusion on his face, "Colt. This is my date," he says in a deep voice that holds a hint of amusement. Pulling me close to him, his eyes light up, "Go snag one of the other bridesmaids," he smiles, pulling me away from Colt as we head back to our table.

I side eye Colt, still standing in place with one hand in a sling and the other clenching and releasing. Without blinking, his eyes never leave Jay as we dance.

Does he know Jay? I never found out what Colt did. I presumed he was in college or nearing graduation. I knew he rode a motorcycle. Could he be in a gang? The same gang Jay is in? I don't remember Macy ever saying what club he was in, but I need to ask her.

"Macy tells me you do consulting work," Jay says, catching me off guard. I was too wrapped up thinking about Colt.

"Hmm. Yes," I utter back, not sure if he's trying to break the tension that filled the air between him and

Colt, but I welcome the distraction. "I just started, so I'm still trying to build up my portfolio."

"We could use your help at work. Are you available to take on more clients right now?" He pulls back, looking at my face, waiting for my response. I eye him suspiciously, because the man has too much of a gleam in his eye.

What is he up to?

"I have time between now and taking a new client in a month," I inform him. "I don't know about helping any more after that, because I've already committed to my new client."

"A month, huh? Well, we could use all the help we could get, especially right now. How about I give you the address and you drop by on Monday around six in the evening?"

I let the thought soak in. I could use the money, especially since I've been going out on my own.

"I could do that. I'm not saying I will take it. I'll only guarantee I'll stop off and get an idea of what you need."

"I have a good feeling about this," he says with a sly, intoxicating grin.

I bet that smile gets him laid, night after night.

We dance the rest of the night, and I haven't spotted Colt, but I'm not surprised because Jay has kept his arm around me for the better part of the night.

"I need to sit down. My feet are killing me," I yell over the music.

Jay grabs my hand and leads me over to where we were sitting during our meal. "I'll go grab you some water."

I watch his back disappear through the large crowd heading to the bar and I slide off my shoes, feeling instant relief. When a familiar smell assaults my nostrils, I close my eyes, inhaling more of Colt's scent. I have missed that masculine musk smell. No one smells like Colt does, and I want nothing more than to get drunk on him.

"Missed me?" His deep, throaty voice whispers in my ear.

I don't answer. If I do, my voice will give me away because his voice alone could make me come.

His hand slides away when Jay comes back with two bottles of water.

Damn him for not taking longer!

Sliding up next to me, Jay opens a water and hands it to me.

"Have you met Colt?" Jay asks.

"We kind of met this summer," I reply, leaving out the details of how he finger fucked me on a float and gave me one hell of an orgasm.

Jay gives us a shit-eating grin. "Is that so?" His voice is filled with amusement. "Colt owns the bar where your help is needed."

My eyes shoot up to Colt with surprise. He owns the bar? Of course, I've seen his dad's lake house. I know they have money and I bet his dad helped him purchase it. Damn spoil rich kids.

"Maggie here is an accountant," Jay says to Colt.

Colt raises his eyebrow.

"She's coming by Monday." Jay takes a drink of his water with his eyes still on Colt. "I'm going to take a ride on my bike afterwards."

Colt's body stiffens harder than a piece of board.

Jay looks around the room, looking for someone. "Oh shit! I'll be right back. I need to give Joel my special gift before they disappear. Don't go anywhere, Maggie," Jay winks, leaving Colt looking like a statue of concrete.

The air between me and Colt is stale, neither one of us speaks until Colt lowers his face down and with his good arm, he puts a death grip on my upper arm, pulling me out of my seat and marches out of the tent and straight into the restroom inside the Hallmark house.

"Let's get one thing straight. You. Won't. Be. On anyone's bike but mine. GOT IT?" He doesn't wait for a response before he slams his lips in mine, demanding entrance with his tongue.

I don't give him access, and he pulls away with a burning fire in his blue eyes that could make me explode into a ball of dust.

"Open that pretty mouth or I'm going to ram my cock in it."

My jaw drops at his provocative words, and he uses that moment to crash his lips to mine, snaking his tongue into my mouth with smooth strokes. My moans are loud at the feel of his hard body pressed up against mine. It's been so long since I've had this fire in my belly, the kind of fire only he can start.

When he pulls away, he nips my bottom lip, then sucks it between his, making my eyes roll closed.

"Fuck, I've missed your taste," he says breathlessly.

Pushing him back with all the strength I can muster, I tell him, "I can't do this again."

"Why?" he asks. "Because of Jay?"

"Yes, he asked me out and I'm not a woman that cheats. I shouldn't have let you..." I stumble over my words, hating them as they spill out of my mouth. "We shouldn't have... you know, at your dad's."

His eyes darken, "I mean what I said. Don't fucking get on his bike." Turning away from me, he opens the door with force and walks out.

Leaving me in shock at how demanding he was. I had no idea he had such a rough side and oddly, I'm turned on more by it.

CHAPTER 8

Colt

I force myself to walk away from Maggie. Her presence with Jay has unnerved me. He didn't mention the woman's name that he asked out, and I did not know it was Maggie. My fucking luck!

Jay's not only my employee but a good friend and a fellow brother in the Fallen Saints MC. Going after another's old lady is a hard no, but she's not his old lady. Even if she's not, I shouldn't have kissed her, but I've been waiting too long to see her again, to taste her. The faint hints of cinnamon still rest on my lips and I want to slide my tongue over every inch of her body, worshipping her.

Fuck it. She was mine before he knew her. Ever since the day I saw those tone tan legs. I don't feel shame or remorse for kissing those fuckable lips. I'm up for the challenge of getting her to beg me for more than just my fingers between her legs.

Leaving now would be a good idea. I'm too worked up, but I'm hoping my drink will calm the fight in me.

Cutting my throat would be easier than watching Maggie with anyone else, but I'm a sucker for punishment. I need to make sure Maggie follows the rule I put in place for her.

When Jay sweeps her into his arms, leading her to the dance floor, I grind my molars. I've never felt this way over a woman. So possessive and out of control over the hold she has on me.

The night finally ends, and the newly happy couple gathers everyone to throw the garter and bouquet. Calling for all the single women to huddle. Macy turns her back to the women, who are laughing and pushing each other. She throws her bundle of flowers, sending it over the heads of some women and it lands in Maggie's hand. My neck heats.

I've got to get that garter.

"All you single men come to the dance floor." Gulping my last sip, I place my glass down and prepare for a battle.

We're waiting as Joel slides the garter off his bride and sling shots it up in the air. Never taking my eyes off it, I jump up and Jay tries to intercept, but I push him with my good shoulder, knocking him down on his ass. Snatching the garter, I grin at my victory.

"You fucking ass," Jay laughs.

Holding my hand out, he takes it, lifting himself up. After the couple says their good byes Maggie says something to Jay and I follow closely when Jay leads her out to her car. When he leans in to make his move, I step up, putting myself between them.

"Drive safe," I grit out between clinch teeth.

Jay's eyes are lit up and I can see right through this fucker. He's playing with fire.

"Maggie, I'll call you later," Jay comments while looking into my eyes.

Reaching down, I open the car door for her and she slides in. We wait for her to drive off, but her car doesn't crank. She has a confused expression and I tap on her window.

Openly her door, I ask her, "Pop the hood and I'll look at it," I'm not a mechanic but I've worked on my share of old cars.

When she unlocks the hood, I raise it, and my eyes widen. "Shit," I whisper.

It's dark but you can see where wires have been cut. What if we hadn't walked her out? What would have happened if she was all alone out here? Could there be someone waiting in the shadows, wanting to harm her? Call it possessiveness, call it overbearing, but she's not going home tonight. Not without me.

"Fuckkk," Jays breathes out beside me. "Could that skinny fucker I showed out the door earlier have done this?"

I shake my head, "I would've told you no before tonight. I've never seen him looking like that. He's always been put together."

"You know him?" Jay asks.

"Step-brother."

He laughs. "Fuck man. What the hell is going on and why haven't you ever mention him before tonight?"

"Nothing to say. We don't get along." I shut the hood and walk over to Maggie's door. "Come on," holding my hand out for her to take, she stares at me, "We'll come back tomorrow, but it's too dark to see what's wrong or fix it right now, plus it's late." Jay nods, agreeing with me.

"I'll take you home," Jay announces.

The hell he will.

"She'll ride with me. That dress is not made to be on the back of a bike and I drove my truck." Taking no chances of Maggie backing out, I grab her hand and pull her to her feet, pulling her toward my truck.

"What the fuck, man? You cockblocking me?" Jay whispers beside me.

After Maggie gets into the truck, I close the door, shrugging my shoulder at Jay.

"She needs more than just your pitiful dick."

He laughs. "Trust me, my large joy stick is anything but pitiful. It's fucking fantastic. Five-star rating!"

"You're a sick motherfucker," I say, walking around to the driver's side.

"See you tomorrow and you can thank me later for finding you help," he yells walking backwards.

"Call one of the guys and get them to tow Maggie's car to Michael's."

"Got it."

***

Maggie gave me her address last night, and I tensed up, knowing Charles had lied about her moving. Did that skinny bastard do that on purpose, or has she been dodging him? I did my best to keep my hands to myself trying to be a gentleman, but fuck, when she had crossed her legs, I just about lost it.

I'm adjusting my cock when a soft knock occurs at my office door. When my eyes cut across the room, they rest on a set of nude heels. My eyes move up to a perfect set of toned legs, inching further up to a blue pencil skirt and a white blouse that's almost see though. I already know what's waiting under that top, the best sets of tits I've ever seen.

"Eyes up here, Romeo," Maggie's voice calls out.

I grin, but then Jay pops out beside her and my grin falls.

"Get your ass back to work," I scold Jay, then throw a stapler in his direction.

"Boys will be boys," Maggie mumbles.

"Come in Maggie." I stand, offering her a seat. "How did you get here?" I ask, curious to find out if someone dropped her off.

"Uber," she says, sitting across from me.

I can see the swell of her breasts. Shit, I can't think when they're calling to me. She snaps her fingers and I know I've been caught again.

"Colt, maybe you should find someone else to help you, or do you really need my help?"

Fuck. I've got to do better than this. I don't want her to leave, not if I'm going to work my magic on her. Ignoring her question, I go on filling her in on what I need and how I'm not balancing things well.

"When can you start?" I wait on the edge of my seat, hoping she'll say yes.

Her eyes search mine, looking for something. I can't help bouncing my knee under my desk, waiting to hear her answer.

She exhales. "This is strictly business, nothing more. I won't be able to stay longer than a month, but hopefully I won't need that long."

What she doesn't know is I'm planning on her staying longer.

"Understood. Can you start today?"

CHAPTER 9

Maggie

The entire time Colt spoke, all I could think about was his lips pressed against mine. That kiss Saturday night sent me home needy and wet. I couldn't doze off until I took care of the issue throbbing between my legs. Now here I sat, engulfed in his scent. Why does he have to smell so good?

Shuffling paper around, I try to place all his bills and receipts in order by date. I'm distracted when I hear a loud commotion down the hall. Sounds of people yelling vibrate through the small office and I peel myself out of the chair, easing toward the door. A man dressed in a black hood jumps from the hallway, blocking the doorway with a gun pointed at me, and I can't stop myself from screaming. The fear of being shot runs like an icy chill through my body.

"Please don't shoot me," I beg the man.

"I've got one in here," he yells out. "Is there

anyone else back here?" The man asks as his eyes search the small office.

"No... no one besides me." I swallow.

Cries and yelling echo down the hall, filling my ears. The man stands aside and points his gun back and forth, instructing me to walk to where all the noise is coming from.

When we reach the end of the hall, there are several men dressed the same, standing around with the word SWAT stretched across their backs.

What the hell has Colt done?

I'm instructed to walk outside and told to sit alongside the other employees. When I spot Colt and Jay, they're handcuffed, sitting against a police car. Colt doesn't make eye contact with me. I can tell he's lost in his thoughts, his face is hard, and his stare is deadly.

Dogs are led inside the bar and what seems like hours pass before the policeman walks out with a small bag in one hand. I listen to their faint whispers. One of them mentions drugs, holding up the sandwich bag, making my stomach flip. Could Colt or Jay be dealing drugs?

I'm briefly interrogated along with the other employees before they let us go free. I'm confused when they release all the employees except for Colt and Jay. How would they know who's drugs they are? Unless, maybe, they've had issues in the past.

When I'm released, I don't waste any time before calling my sister to come and pick me up.

Jessica arrives twenty minutes later and I all but jump into her car. She pinches her brows together, "Thanks for picking me up."

Her eyes scan the parking lot filled with SWAT teams and police cars, "What the hell is happening?"

"No one has really said anything, but I think it has something to do with drugs. They asked me questions like how long had I known Colt or Jay, and what was I doing in the back. Of course, I told them I was doing some consulting work for Colt, but the policeman just gave me a look as if I was guilty. Me!" I place my hand on my chest. "I can tell you one thing, I won't be back," I spill out to Jessica.

I need a stiff drink.

"Do you think he's guilty?"

Her question makes me think. What do I truly know about him? Does he seem like the kind of person that would get involved with such nonsense? It doesn't make sense to keep something at his business. He seemed to have a lot of pride in his bar. I wouldn't have thought someone that worked that hard at getting his establishment started would jeopardize it, but then again, drugs make you do all sorts of stupid stuff.

"I don't know," I murmur.

The next day, I decide to clean my apartment. I don't plan ongoing back to work for Colt, and the possibility of him being in jail means I doubt he'll call me. Around lunch time, the doorbell rings and I stare at the front door, scared to cross the room, waiting to see if a team of men will come busting in. The shock of last night's events has scarred me. When the bell rings again, my heart races, and I find myself walking toward the front door as fast as a sloth.

Peeping out the peephole, I don't see anyone. Going on my tiptoes, I press my face up closer to the door, trying to see if I can see down the hallway. Maybe it's some brat playing a prank, but no one is in sight.

I've watched horror movies before and usually the person opens the door only to get overpowered and killed, but I'm not a dumb bunny and this isn't the movies. There's no way in hell I'm opening that door. Stepping back, my eyes stay focused on the door until a loud bang erupts, causing me to fly backwards. *What the —.*

"Maggie, open the door. I know you're in there," Colt yells from the other side, giving my door one more bang, shaking the door violently.

"Just a damn minute. You don't have to let the whole building know you're here," the last thing I need is Ms. Putman across the hall trying to get in my business.

Unlocking the door, Colt flies in my apartment. His hair stands up in a ruffled mess, with eyes that are bloodshot, as if he hasn't slept in days. I catch a glimpse of a purple sweater and I cringe. Ms. Putman's favorite cat sweater is purple and when I do a double take, sure enough, she's peeping around her door frame.

Just great!

"Sorry," I tell her. "Everything is okay, nothing to worry about," I apologize, slamming my door. I cross my arms and stalk over to Colt.

"What the hell, Colt! You can't bang on my door like that. Someone will call the police."

He huffs, pacing the floor.

My patience is wearing down, just like he's wearing down the carpet in my living room. Having enough of his bull, I yell out, "Are you going to say something, or just wear the threads in my carpet down?"

He stops with his back to me. Slow and easy, he turns his head in my direction. I feel intimidated as I watch his muscles in his jaws twitch. Straightening himself upright, he finally speaks.

"Did you plant drugs in my office?"

Speechless. He's left me freaking speechless. I'm there for one day and he thinks I would do something so despicable.

Annoyed at his accusations, I scream at him, "How dare you come into my apartment and accuse me of something that only a low life would do. You can get the hell out!" I storm toward the front door, but his large hands grab me and throws me on the couch. He sits on top of my legs, holding me down.

I scream, balling my hands into fists as I start pounding against his chest. There's no use. His sadistic smile tells me he's enjoying me fighting him. He grabs my wrists, hauling them above my head. My chest heaves with fury.

"Careful, pussycat. You might hurt yourself," he laughs and shit, it goes straight to my core. "Give me a minute to finish what I was saying," he looks down at my chest rising and falling while I'm trying to catch my breath. "Fuck, your tits are the perfect pair," his eyes meet mine and I can see desire swirling around in them. Licking his lips he speaks, but his eyes flick down to my chest again, "What I was saying—"

"Eyes up here when you're talking. The girls won't talk back." I smart off.

He smiles, "Pussycat. Listen," *Silence.* "Do you hear them? They're talking to me. Begging me to pull them out."

"Colt," I struggle against his hold. "I'm not playing. Don't come in here and accuse me of something and then try to woo me."

He shrugs his shoulders, "You can't blame me for trying." His tongue darts out, licking his bottom lip. "They are truly fuckable." Putting a serious face on, he continues, "What I'm trying to say and maybe I should have done it better, is that I don't do drugs and since you were the last person in my office, I only thought it might have been your stash."

"Get off me," he pulls his hands back, holding them up as he lifts his big beautiful body off me, adjusting his cock.

I roll my eyes. "They weren't mine. I've never even touched pot, much less anything else." I huff out.

Colt sits down at my feet, and I scramble up to go

sit in the chair across from him. I don't trust myself with him. He's way better looking than I remember and fuck, it's been too long since I've had sex.

He runs his hand through his hair. Exhaustion settles over his body like a blanket. He throws his head back, resting it on my couch as he exhales.

"Have you slept?" I ask, my voice is soft.

He shakes his head.

Arguing with him is hot and makes my core throb with want, but when he looks lost and defeated. All I want is to help make things better. This man does something to me. I feel a connection with him I've never felt with anyone else.

"I don't know who or why drugs were put in your office... maybe you should have your employees drug tested. It would make good sense that you establish now that you won't put up with anyone doing drugs... that is, if you don't do drugs," my voice trails off, hoping not to make him upset.

His eyes pin me, putting a choke hold on my lungs. Hurt crosses his face, making me angry at my no filter mouth. I've always had a mouth that could make the Pope pissed. My mother said that was my best feature, but it didn't help when making new friends.

"What would make you think I would do drugs?" He asks and I can tell I've hit a nerve.

Playing with the thread on the worn out chair I'm sitting in, I inform him, "If you're friends with Jay, then I thought you might be in the same motorcycle gang. I hear all the time how MC gangs do drugs."

He laughs. "You can't believe everything you hear or see on television. Don't you know they make that shit up just to get better ratings? My brothers and I don't do drugs."

A burn spreads from my neck to my cheeks, filled with embarrassment that I automatically thought of him as someone that would do drugs. I'm relieved that he wouldn't be involved in drugs. I can't see why you would work so hard on your body only to hurt it with drugs, especially with a body like Colt's.

Colt's phone rings, sliding it out of his pocket, he inhales then whispers under his breath.

"It's my dad. I've got to take this," standing up, he walks to my small kitchen.

My apartment doesn't leave much room for privacy. The kitchen is basically open to the living room. So, when Colt paces in my kitchen. I watch him trying to listen in on his conversation. I guess Ms. Puttman isn't the only nosey person.

CHAPTER 10

Colt

"Where are you?" my dad ask as urgency rings out in his loud voice. The sounds of cars rushing by are playing in the background and I know he's not in his office.

My eyes skip over to Maggie, skimming down her body. She's wearing shorts and a tank top. The bright sunlight beams through her living room, shining through the thin material and giving an outline of the swell of her breasts. It's a sight that would make men crumble. The view makes my dick pulse up against my zipper. Damn, she looks good.

"Colt!" my dad's voice screams into the phone. Whispering under his breath, I hear his words, "Fuck. What in the hell is going on?"

That's when I realize he must be at the bar. It's rare he'll show up there, and the thought of him being there sends me into worrying that something is wrong. When Jay and I were dropped off this morning at my place, I jumped on my bike and headed straight over to Maggie's, needing to confront her. Knowing that she was the last person in my office and that's where they found the drugs, I was eaten up with rage and couldn't drive fast enough to make it over. A part of me was hoping she hadn't planted the drugs. I just hope she isn't lying to keep the heat off her.

"Are you at the bar?" I ask to confirm my suspicion.

"I showed up thinking we could have a talk, but you're not here. What's going on? It's not like you to not be here."

It would be best I tell him in person about the drug raid. I let him know I'm on my way. Once I hang up, I glance at Maggie. I need to stay calm and figure out who pulled this crap. Maybe it's time to start random drug testing my employees. Although, what they do in their own time is their business, but when it comes to bringing that shit to work with them? That makes it my business.

"I need you at work by five tonight," I say, glaring at Maggie as I watch her swallow nervously. Her face is set in hard lines and I can tell she wants to walk away, but I be damn if I let her.

"No, I don't know what is going on, and I want nothing to do with it. You'll have to find someone else," she states as she winds up the cord to her vacuum.

"Maggie," I stalk over to her, but she steps

backwards, trying to avoid me. When the back of her legs hit the coffee table. She starts to fall backwards, but I take a gigantic step to grab her, catching her before she flys into the glass top. I pull her upright and into my chest and her minty breath fans my face. Fuck me. I've never been so effective by a woman's breath.

"Maggie," I whisper. My heart is racing from the need to kiss her. "Trust me when I tell you I. Don't. Do drugs, I wouldn't touch them. Look at me," I flex my pecks, hoping to break some of the tension in her body. "Do I look like I would mess up this body with that mess?" I say with a cocky grin.

Her eyes turn to angry slits, but I know she appreciates my body. I've caught her on more than one occasion checking me out.

"I need you…" I want to tell her how I feel, but Jay's name keeps popping up in my mind and I can't betray my friend like that. "To help me with my office work," *among other things*. I leave out the last part because she'll find out sooner than later what I really need help with. I just need to figure out how to break the news to Jay that I claimed her first. "I would never put you in a difficult position unless you wanted to be posed that way," I wink. "What do you say? Come back?" I wait patiently for her reply, hoping she'll say she will.

With a huff, she finally answers, "Yes, but if it happens again? I'm out. I won't be back."

Placing a kiss to her forehead, I breathe a sigh of

relief. *Maybe there's still a chance I can save my reputation along with my business.*

"I've got to head out, but I'll see you tonight, right?" I ask, wanting confirmation again. She nods, sending my heart into rapid beats.

***

Parking my bike, I swing my leg over and pull off my helmet. Dad's large stature leans against the front door, waiting with the patience that's still developing in me. All my life, people have always said I look identical to him. It's only the last few years that I've filled out to match his size.

"Want a drink?"

"A bit too early for a drink, isn't it?" he asks with questioning eyes.

I grunt. If he only knew the night, I've had. Being held in jail overnight only for a bag of weed that wasn't large enough to count for possession with the intent to sell was bullshit. There's no way they just sprung that raid. Someone had to tip them off, but who? Who would be stupid enough to go against me? A shiver runs up my spine, making me twist my neck to release the tension of last night from my mind.

Pulling myself back to my dad's question, I finally answer him, "It's afternoon, no harm in a drink at this time of the day."

When I round the bar, I pull a bottle of scotch off the shelf and two glasses, filling them to the brim. I pass his across the bar and throw mine back then set it up again. I watch how he swirls his drink in his hand, looking at it with a desolate stare.

"Do you want to tell me what you are doing out here during the day and not at work?"

Work is something dad has always taken seriously. I can't remember the last time he took off for a vacation or just to have time off. So I know something is bothering him. Especially with the way he's eyeing his drink like he would prefer to drown himself in it. His chest rises as he sucks in the air around us but when he releases it, his sad eyes meet mine.

"You know one day soon I had hoped to retire," he swallows. "Doesn't appear that's going to happen," he drains the last of his drink.

My brows furrow. I know he's always thought of an early retirement. That's why he's been saving and skipping out on so many extra pleasures. Doesn't mean my stepmother Connie does. She uses my dad's money to throw in front of everyone, always buying the latest in clothes, electronics, and cars. She redecorates their house every year wearing their bank account thin on the outrageous remodels.

"Dad, what are you talking about? You've been putting money back for years."

He squeezes his eyes shut and rubs his forehead, swiping back and forward. He opens his mouth but closes it as if he's trying to decide what to tell me. I wait for him to speak in his own time. Fear strikes me as I imagine what he's going to say next.

"Have you spoken to Charles lately?" I narrow my

eyes. He's trying to change the subject.

"Is this about Charles? Or are you changing the subject?" I refuse to believe he took the day off and came all the way out of here to talk about that piece of crap.

Defeat settles in his eyes, and I avoid arguing with him. He'll tell me when he's ready. "What has he asked for this time?" Charles is just as bad as Connie, always wanting or needing money, but they never want to repay it. I slam my drink down, pissed off, as I remember how much money Charles has borrowed from my dad.

"Connie hasn't heard from him in a few weeks. She's worried. She says he's been acting strange lately and thinks he might need to take a vacation to get himself together."

I laugh. It comes out dark.

"He needs to grow up," I state as a fact, and my dad doesn't argue. "Is that why you don't feel like you can retire in a few years?"

He exhales and I grip the edge of the butcher block countertop, praying that he's not the reason or I'll kill him.

"No...," dad exhales. "I...," he stalls. "I found out Connie has an extremely God awful amount of debt. I'm not talking about a debt that you get from running a credit card, up I'm talking going behind your back and buying jewelry that cost more than my mortgage," muttering under his breath he says, "I shouldn't be talking about this with you."

My blood boils. *Fucking bitch.*

"Are you leaving her?" The question hangs in the air as he takes his time to answer. After a long pause, he nods. My first thought is she's going to ring him dry. I was just a kid when they married, but I can't help but ask, "Did you get a prenup?" He nods again, and I relaxed, knowing that he'll be safe from her blood drawing claws.

I pour him another drink and we sit in silence until the front door opens. We both swing our heads to see Kaitlyn walking in. My dad sits up straighter, and I see a spark of interest in his eyes when they land on my new assistant manager.

"Kaitlyn," she glances up from her cell phone with a faint smile and I motion her over. When she glances over to the barstool where my dad is currently perched, I feel the electricity of her interest. Standing back to not get shocked by the bolts of heat between them, I introduce her. "This is my dad, Connor Donovan. This is Kaitlyn Myers. She's my new assistant manager."

They greet each other and when they reach out to shake hands; I count the seconds they hold on to each other, one, two..., six. *Shit. Let go already.*

"Connor," I say his name to pull him out of the lustful state he's in. "Connor," when he comes back to the moment, he slowly drops her hand and I shake my head.

Grabbing my keys and helmet, I let Kaitlyn know I'm stepping out. I yank my dad up and have to push him out of the bar, letting the door slam behind us. I lower my voice when I say, "Not until you're free, old man," I tease, laughing to myself as when I walk around my bike.

"I'm only forty-five. I'm not fucking old," he argues.

CHAPTER 11

Maggie

Reapplying my lipstick in my mirror, I breathe in
before opening my car door. Nerves are a bitch! My
hand trembles when I reach for the doorknob.

*Breathe Maggie. He's hot as fuck and makes you want to
get down on your knees, but stay calm.*

When I walk inside, Jay meets me at the door,
"Maggie, you're looking..." his eyes rake me in over,
but it doesn't affect me the same way as Colt's eyes do.
"Good."

Smiling at his comment, I give him a settle,
"Thanks."

"Maybe this weekend we can go out on that date,"
he winks.

Fuck! A part of me was hoping he would have
forgotten. No chance. Just my luck! I put on my best
fake smile. Glass shatters in the distance, and I see Colt
standing behind the bar with a murderous look on his

face. He's not looking at his friend. He's looking at me. Being the rebel I am, I give my attention back to Jay.

"That sounds great!" I say to his offer, raising my voice for Colt to hear. "Have you been to that new restaurant, Crystal Clear? It's supposed to be a dark mood setting atmosphere. Maybe we can try it out?" I say with a little more of a rough voice.

Jay's eyes widen and for a split second I see them divert over to Colt, then back to me. He quickly affixes a smirk on his full lips.

Interesting.

"Sounds… like a date," he announces with amusement. He glances over at Colt before walking over to a table where apparently someone has had more to drink than they can handle.

"Maggie," Colts calls with a gruff voice. "Follow me," he leads us down the small hallway to his office.

That's where I was going anyway. I tell myself.

After I enter, he slams the door behind me, caging me up against a filing cabinet.

"Do you think you can stop flirting with Jay? I don't need my employees distracted," he growls at me.

Seriously?

My heart races at his tone.

"He's the one that stopped me!" I poke him in the chest. "If anyone is distracting anyone from working, it would be you. You're standing here giving me a lecture when I should be working." I lay my hand against his chest and push him out of my way.

He grabs my arm, turns me around, and stares into my eyes, "Call off your date with Jay," his voice is loaded with a fury of fire.

"I don't think I will. I'm going on that date." My voice comes out stern.

Instead of pressing me any further, a vengeful scheme lights up behind those grey eyes. Saying nothing else, he leaves the office. I'm left to wonder why he didn't press me more about ending the date. Does he think the silent treatment will make me let him have his way?

After working continuously for the past several hours, I stop, needing to stretch my legs and grab a soda. I head to the bar. When I enter the area, that's filled with loud chatter, I spot Colt. A blonde chick is clinging to him like a piece of lint. She's attractive, in a biker chick way. Her skirt is short enough to show her vajayjay if she bent over just right. I'm sure that's just what she's hoping to be bent over by Colt. Just the thought of Colt bending someone over makes my nails dig into my palm.

As if he feels my presence, his eyes swing over to collide with mine. A perfect smirk crosses that god like face, and I curse how good looking he is. Is he trying to make me jealous by letting her hang onto him like that? Because I'm not the least bit concerned if he bends her over the bar stool right now. Okay, that's a lie. I quickly look away, not wanting to give him the pleasure of seeing the ugly green-eyed monster coming out in me. Planting my ass on a barstool, I motion to the bartender for a soda.

Jay grabs the barstool next to me, wrapping his thick thighs around the seat until his butt slides in place. If I wasn't so infatuated with Colt, I might find him attractive. He's good looking and well built, but there's nothing there that screams I want him, not the way I want Colt. My body calls out to him like no one else. It scares me how my body reacts to him.

"Taking a break?" Jay asks.

I take a sip of my coke.

"Yeah, I needed to stretch my legs."

"Jay," Colt steps up beside his friend with a cocky grin. The blonde bimbo is still hanging onto his arm. "Want to make your date with Maggie a double date?"

I spit out my drink, spraying it across the bar and the bartender. *Poor guy.*

A hand pats my back, and I hear the blond snicker. "That was classy."

Fucking bitch.

"I guess it's about as classy as wearing a skirt that would fit my two-year-old niece," I lie. I don't have a niece.

Jay laughs.

I'm just hoping he'll tell Colt no, but nope, he doesn't.

"I was hoping to sweep Maggie off her feet and out of her pants. Don't know if I'll be able to do it with you there," Jay winks at me. "But I guess that could make the night even more interesting. Do you plan on taking her?" Jay points to the bimbo. "Or are you taking another chick?"

The blonde gasps as if she can't believe not everyone would find her presence annoying. Colt nods and my stomach threatens to lurch everything back up that I've eaten today.

I grab my coke and get up off the barstool, "I need to get back at it," I wave to Jay, telling him bye and ignore Colt and the slut hanging onto him.

***

Three hours later, it's ten o'clock and I'm ready to head out. I stuff my large tote with all my belongings and everything else that I will need to work from home for the next few days. It might be best if I find a way to work at a distance until I can figure out a way to end this dreaded double date that Colt has forced up on me.

Jerking the tote up along with my purse, I push the back door open to go to my car. I'll text him when I get in the car that I've left and won't need to come back for a few days. When the door shuts with a slam behind me, it makes me jump, an uneasy feeling settling in my gut.

The back parking lot is dark. Goosebumps rise along my body, and I suppress the feeling that I'm not alone as I hurry to my car. The sound of gravel crunching makes my breathing pick up and I high step it to the back of the lot where my car is parked at the edge where it's the darkest.

My car is almost within reach when I pick up the pace, running to it. I hold up my fob to unlock my door. When I turn in the space between my car and the next, my ankle twists causing me to almost fall. Steadying myself on the car beside mine, I barely make out the word spray painted on my car. *Whore.* My heart races in disbelief. Numbness runs through my legs, but hands grip my shoulders as I scream, not sure if it's the sight of my car or if it's the hands that pull me back into a chest. I thrust my arms when a man's lips brush over my ear.

"I've got you," he whispers. "Calm down Maggie," Colt wraps his hands around me, bracing me from hurting him or myself with the way I was throwing punches. "Are you okay?" I nod. "I'm going to let you go now."

He slowly loosens his grip, and his hands linger on my arms till they disappear, leaving me cold and craving their warmth.

"Who did this?" I ask in a whisper, not even able to hear myself properly with how quietly I ask the question.

Colt walks around my car, looking to see if there's any more damage. When he exhales, I feel the disappointment of knowing someone has damaged the passenger side, too. I pull out my cell phone and dial the police.

"What are you doing?" Colt's ask with cold eyes.

"I'm calling the police to file a report. Someone damaged my car, in-case you've forgotten."

Colt walks back over to me and snatches my phone from me.

"You can't do that. They'll be all over the bar. I don't need them being here more than they have been already."

"What am I supposed to do? Ride around with *Whore* spray painted on my car?"

He doesn't answer. Instead, he pulls his cell out, punching a number in, "Cutter," I hear loud music in the background. "Come to The Mule. I need you to bring Shadow with you," he hangs up.

"I'll get it taken care of. I just need you to trust me."

"How am I supposed to get home?" I look at my car, feeling hurt that someone would commit such an act against me. I could call my sister, but I don't want her to worry and call our parents. My mom would go into one of her many panic attacks, worrying about her daughters who live out on their own. I'm not ready to hear how I need to move back in with them.

"Something is going on and I don't like it one bit. First the drugs planted in my bar, and now your car being vandalized. I don't think it would be good for you to be by yourself."

"I'll be fine. I plan on working a few days at home, so I won't be coming back until I can get all your paperwork recorded. Maybe they just got my car mixed up with someone else," I tell him.

Even I don't believe the words that leave my mouth. They couldn't have gotten my car mixed up with someone else when it's parked in the back parking lot, tucked away from being seen. It had to be on purpose, but who would do such a thing? Charles? No, it's not in him, or at least I don't think it is. Maybe the slut Colt was parading around? But how would she know what I drive?

"What were you doing out here?" I ask Colt, curious how he got here so fast.

"The back door alarm went off on my phone. I was already outside, so I ran around the building to see who it was. I didn't think you would leave out the back door," Colt points up at the light someone busted. "When I came around and realized the light was busted, something didn't feel right."

What was he doing outside?

"Do you think that happened tonight?" My voice sounds a little broken when I ask Colt.

"I know what you're doing. You're trying to get out of what I'm telling you. You're not going home, not unless I go with you. Let's go back inside. I'll take you home to check things out. I need to tell Jay I'm leaving and wait on Cutter to get here. I'll have your car fixed for you."

"I can take care of myself—"

He steps into my bubble. My nose almost presses up against his chest. Putting his forefinger under my chin, he raises my face to meet his. A muscle ticks in his jaw, and I can see I might be riding a fine line, but I've never been one to back down.

"I didn't say you couldn't. You're going to go back inside and wait on me. Do you want me to carry you, or are you going to be a good girl and walk through that door?"

I swallow the lump in my throat. He's serious. His expression gives no room for argument.

CHAPTER 12

Colt

The thought of someone hurting Maggie sends red-hot coals sinking into my stomach, making my blood sears my veins as it pumps its way to my heart. I've never wanted to protect anyone as much as I want to protect her. This feeling is more than lust, and standing to the side while she goes out with another man doesn't sit well. She's mine, and it's about time I let her know it.

I will end that damn date with Jay, without coming across like an ass to my friend. Telling him she's mine and there's no way in hell she'll be going out with him might not be the best idea, but it's the only one I can come up with. Respect and honesty would be the most effective way to keep the peace. There's also the fact I watched Jay flirt with every cunt that came in tonight. Never giving his date with Maggie a second thought as his fingers slid under the hem of their tops. If he was determined to make Maggie his, he wouldn't have been fingering the girl I caught him with earlier tonight in the storage room.

I walked Maggie back to my office, telling her I'd be ready in a few minutes before heading to the lounge, where I can make sure everything is handled before I skip out for the night.

"Jay, I need you to close up tonight," I yell from behind the bar. He's standing up against it with his back to me as he watches the crowd.

Counting the bottles of liquor, I'm happy with what is in stock for the rest of the night. I don't want to leave my staff in a bind where they have to leave the bar. Sometimes we get a rush of people between midnight and two a.m. and it's best if things are in arm's reach instead of them having to walk away.

He grins like he thinks I'm slipping off to go fuck someone. If I get what I want, I know, I'll be sliding my dick in that perfect pussy of hers in no time. But tonight won't be the night. She's too upset and I'm not one to use a woman, especially someone like Maggie, when they're in distress.

Before he has time to open his mouth, Cutter and Shadow waltz in. They greet Jay, then head over my way.

"What's up? Who's ass we need to kick?" Cutter asks, looking over the heads of the people lingering in the bar.

Shaking my head at him, I tell them, "I need you to drive one of my employees' cars to the shop. It was vandalized tonight. It's out back," he gives me a nod, letting his eyes roam over the crowd one more time.

"Serena here?"

"No. You still panting over her?"

"She said she was coming to hang out with friends."

"Shit man, she's probably sucking some random guy off," his jaw ticks. Jay has gotten too close to Serena. Lusting after her, she's going to cause him nothing but trouble. "Come on. We'll go out the back. I need to grab Maggie's keys from her."

When we walk into the small hallway that heads to my office, the door is open, and I see Maggie bent over giving me a perfect view of her round ass. I glance over and see Cutter's tongue all but hanging to his collarbone, making me ball my hand up.

"Maggie," yelling her name startles her. She jumps up, straightening her back. "I need the keys to your car."

"Fuckkk," Cutter says under his breath.

"Don't fucking look at her," I growl.

He laughs, "Possessive much?"

He has no idea.

Keys in hand, we walk out back where Cutter gets behind the wheel and drives Maggie's car to the paint shop the club owns, letting Shadow follow him. Thank fuck the guys weren't on a run when I called them to come help me out. I've never had any incidents like this happening at The Mule before. There's a first time for everything, but I'm eager to look at the video surveillance. With the light being busted, I'm not sure if I'll be able to see anything, anyway. I really should get more lighting added for security.

Maggie's quiet the entire drive back to her house. The only noise in the truck is from her shuffling in the seat. Gently placing her hand in mine, I rub my thumb over her knuckles, trying to help release the tension in her body.

"I'm coming up with you I want you to grab a bag and stay with me," I announce.

"I'll be fine. I'll just stay inside for the night. I'm sure it was a mistake. Someone mistook my car for someone else," she still has concern etches into the lines of her face. I know she's lying to herself.

"Do you believe the words as they come out?"

She doesn't answer me. Instead, she looks out of her window, watching the night go by. I'm grateful for her not jerking away, the small circle motions on my thumb seems to help with the tension in her body.

We pull up at her apartment complex and I drive behind the building to park in the parking lot "Fuck, it's dark out here. Why don't they have it more lit up?" Maggie shrugs her shoulders, like she's used to it.

"Thank you for the ride home," she says when she's about halfway out of out my truck.

Grabbing her wrist, I give it a little squeeze, "You're going inside to grab a bag and then you're coming home with me or... I can stay with you. You choose." She's not getting away from me so quickly, not after what just happened.

She takes a long moment before she rolls her eyes and scoffs at me. "Fine, you can stay with me."

Damn right.

There's not a door to enter the building from the back. So, we have to walk through the alley to the front of the complex. There's an underground parking lot for residents but without her decal, I'm not able to park in it. I wasn't thinking I would be needing it, since I had planned on taking her back to the clubhouse. Throwing her in my bed sounded so good, but her bed would be fine as long her legs still end up wrapped around my shoulders.

We're about halfway down the alley when a rustling noise happens to my left. Pushing Maggie behind me, I angle my body, ready to fight someone off if I need to. Maggie grabs her cell phone and turns on the flashlight, pointing toward the sound. A homeless man is sitting beside the dumpster, trying to uncover a left-over hamburger. Lacing my fingers with hers, I tug at her to keep us moving.

"Tell me you always use the underground parking deck," my voice comes out gruff.

"Yes," she says, breathless with the effort of trying to keep up with me.

"Thank fuck!" I'm pleased to hear she doesn't walk the alley by herself.

When I walk into her apartment, I'm hit with the familiar scent of lavender and vanilla assaulting my nose. It's her signature smell. Inhaling, more of the air, my dick gets hard. I reach down, giving it a tight squeeze. Maggie's eyes go wide.

"Your scent is making me hard as a fucking rock," I can't stop myself when I intertwine my fingers into the waves of her golden hair. It's being in her space that has my head clouded with arousal. I tilt her head back slightly and nip at her chin. Reaching out to her hand, I place it on my dick, "This is all yours. Tell me, do you think of me when you touch yourself? Do you think about my tongue lapping up your slit?" Her breaths come out is heavy pants. "If I reach into your panties would my hand be soaked by your needy pussy? I know Charles didn't know how to take care of that pussy like it deserves."

Her throat slowly works up and down as she swallows. Maybe, she's trying to find the words to lie about how she doesn't need me to take care of her. Maybe, she's going to defend that sorry excuse of a stepbrother of mine, but I don't give her time before I slam my lips into hers.

Her moans of pleasure gets swallowed up by my kiss. I grab the front of her shirt, ripping it open. Small buttons fly though the air, scattering across the room. She gasps as if she can't believe I just ripped it. That I would be so desperate to have her naked under me.

"Don't even start with that sassy mouth of yours," I give her a warning. As much as I love battling with her, I want her naked. I need it. I've waited too long to be with her.

"Wait," she puts her hand to my chest. "What about Jay?"

Shit! She's right. It's not like Charles, where I could give a shit less what he thought. Jay's my friend but after seeing him tonight, I doubt he's serious about Maggie.

"I'll text him," gripping her chin, I bring her face back to mine. Pressing our lips together so I can drink more of her. I kiss her with everything in me. She doesn't resist, but she breaks the kiss to soon, leaving me wanting more. Her face turns serious and I know she's about to open that smart mouth again.

"That's petty and shitty. I'm not doing that. Would you want someone to do that to you?" Damn. That's the reason why she was way too good for Charles. She thinks of others, and that's something he never has done. She pulls her hand back from my dick.

I bet her hand would feel even better without the material between us.

"You're right. I'll tell him tomorrow, but I have a slight problem tonight," her brows draw together.

"What?"

"My dick."

Maggie rolls her eyes at my comment about my dick. I wasn't kidding. My cock has been throbbing and waiting patiently for her sweet pussy for too long.

She throws the blanket draped over the couch at me and walks to a hall closet, pulling out a pillow, "Here, you can sleep on the couch."

CHAPTER 13

Colt

The next morning, Maggie promised me she wouldn't leave her apartment unless she texted me. She won't admit it, but I can tell last night spooked her. I know she didn't sleep, because I heard her toss and turn in her bed all night. It was hard to sleep on her sofa when she was half naked in the room next door. Fantasies of her being naked and under me played through my mind all night.

I walk into the clubhouse, expecting it to be empty at this time in the morning. All the men usually work a nine-to-five job with the exception of a few who look after side businesses for the club. J-Bird is our president. He's in charge of the strip clubs, paint shops, and some illegal businesses that are left unspoken.

"Colt," J-Bird tilts his head when I walk into the kitchen. He's sitting at the table eating a plate full eggs, bacon, and pancakes. Shadow, Jay, and Cutter sit along with him at the table with their plates already cleaned. These guys only know how to make one killer meal and it's breakfast.

Propping myself against the countertop I lean over and swipe a piece of bacon off J-Birds plate.

"Fucker, get your own," he tries to stab me with his fork.

"You know you're not supposed to mess with a man's plate," Cutter snickers.

"Clearly," I agree, but it doesn't stop me trying for another piece.

"Where did you stay last night?" Cutter smirks, and the hairs on my neck stand up.

If Maggie was any other woman, I'd be bragging about how I made a woman scream my name while she came undone on my cock, but she's not. I try to ignore Cutter's question for now.

"Someone's fucking around at The Mule," I spit it out like a bad taste in my mouth.

"We heard about the drug raid," J-Bird say between chews. "I've asked my contacts within the police department, and no one knows anything. Thank fuck whoever did it was dumb enough not to put the right amount in your desk to really amount to anything."

"But still. It pisses me off it happened," I push away from the counter. "Last night an employee's car was vandalized," I pace the floor. "I'm not sure who the target is, me or them. It could even be two different individuals for all I know."

"Could it be this employee?" J-Bird questions.

"Who's car?" Jay asks.

Fuck! The last thing I want to do is give him a reason to go and see Maggie. Call me an ass, but I don't want any other man near her.

I grit my teeth, "Maggie," it comes out with a growl.

"Why didn't you tell me?" Jay asks.

Because she didn't need you, she needed me.

"I took care of things," I try to squash any further questions about Maggie. "Keep me informed if you hear anything. I want to make this person pay for fucking with my business," J-Bird eyes me. It's a silent understanding we have. Once I get his answer, I walk out heading to my room. I need a shower.

Heavy footsteps follow behind me. When I unlock my door, I leave it open knowing Jay is behind me. Like I predicted he walks in, shutting the door behind him. Leaning against it, he gives me a look that would frighten most men, but not me.

"Where did you stay last night," his no bullshit attitude comes out.

This is it the moment I need to tell him. He may be pissed, but he'll get over it. Either way I need to tell him she's been mine since this summer.

"Maggie's," I answer him while I throw my pants in my hamper.

"Do you have something you need to tell me?" His voice is even.

"She's mine, Jay. I met her over the summer at my dad's house. She was dating Charles, but it didn't stop me from wanting her, and it doesn't stop me from wanting her now. I wasn't going to step in but then her car got messed with," I drop my head exhaling a loud sigh.

Jay exhales, "I knew you had a thing for her. I could tell at Joel's wedding. I've been fucking with you ever since," he laughs. "I love to see how you react when I screw with you over her."

"Are we good?" I ask, to confirm he's not going to be pissed.

"More than good. I just enjoy fucking with you," he grins, and it makes me feel better knowing that we won't have to fight it out over Maggie. "Maggie's hot don't get me wrong, but I wasn't invested from the beginning. I was just seeing if there was... anything that could be there."

"Alright, now get out, I need to get a shower," he leaves wiggling his eyebrows.

***

I arrive at work a little earlier than normal. I wanted to check on the progress Shadow is making. He's usually gone by the time I get here.

I walk up the steps to my apartment, hearing moaning when I get two steps away from the door. Fuck, don't tell me I'm walking in to see his naked grizzly ass. Knocking on the door before I open it, I yell out wanting to give him a warning, so he'll put his dick away, "Coming in." Opening the door, I'm surprised to see he's putting up sheetrock instead of being inside someone, "What was that moaning I heard?"

He smirks, "This chick sent me a video of her fucking herself," he laughs, taking his phone out. "You want to see?"

"No," I hold my hand up. "I'm good," the only woman I want to see doing that is Maggie.

He slides the phone back into his pocket, "I didn't recognize the number when I opened it, or I wouldn't have bothered viewing it. I'm not into chicks that send videos like that."

"Yeah... well... with a dick like yours they all want a piece," I laugh but I've had unfortunate firsthand experience with seeing his dick. It would put the biggest of stallions to shame. Changing the subject, I tell him, "It's looking good," I'm more than pleased with the work Shadow is doing.

Shadow takes his gloves off, picks up a box and shows it to me, "I got you a security system, state of the art. I thought it would come in handy since you're going to be living above the bar. Everything that's been going on, you need a better security. Cameras will go inside the bar, your office, and the stairway to the apartment. We can change the crappy cameras outside to this system. It has a better night vision so when the streetlights are out, you won't have a problem with getting footage. I picked it up after we talked this morning."

I slapped Shadow on the shoulder, "Thanks for

looking out for me. When can we get this going? May need it sooner rather than later."

"Anytime. I'll start on it tomorrow. I've got to head out to do some estimates for a new potential client."

After Shadow leaves, I call Maggie to check in and make sure she's staying true to her word. Her phone rings twice before she picks it up.

"Hello," her sweet voice sings in my ear.

"Hey pussycat," my voice comes out deep, vibrating down my chest, waking my dick up.

"Colt?"

"Who else? There better not be any other man calling you," I growl out giving her a warning.

"There's only one man in my life and his name is Brody,"

What the fuck!

"If *Brody* valves his health, he needs to take a hike and if I see you with someone, I'm going to kill them and punish you," I snarl.

"Did you call for a reason?" she snaps.

"Are you home?"

"Yes, is that the only reason, why you're calling me? To try to keep me under lock and key? I've got a lot to do and don't have time for your over active testosterone. In case you forgot, I already promised to start with a new client in a week." *Click.*

Did she just hang up on me? Pulling my phone back from my ear I look at the screen. Yep, she did. This woman is going to be a challenge, and I'm down for it.

The minutes turn into hours and before I realize how late it is; the bar becomes eerily quiet. The hairs on my neck stand up when the front door creaks open, and a familiar boot that's laced up the front steps in. Nina. She walks in with a bald man with a skull tattoo on the side of his neck. The skull tattoo is the logo of our rival gang, Deadly Skins.

I haven't seen him around before, and I wonder if he knows this bar is owned by one of the Fallen Saints. He's not a bright man if he's with Nina. Nina's sharp eyes survey the room, looking for trouble. She's always been into drama, and my gut tells me she's trying to get shit started by bringing a member of the Deadly Skins here.

"What's your poison?" I glare at Nina for longer than I should, but I want to let her know there's a no tolerance rule that she shouldn't mess with.

"Jack and coke. What about you darling?" the gang member asks her.

She smirks at me, "Same thing," she says as she leans in to him, trying to wrap herself around him. If she was a man, I would have already knocked the hell out of her.

"Coming up," I head back to the bar and nod my head at Jay for him to watch over them. The last thing I need is for her to start a fight and get this place trashed just because she's got it out for me.

After delivering their drinks to their table, I watch them from the bar while Jay stakes them out while he walks around the room. Their quiet, not really speaking to each other but the feeling of a shit storm coming doesn't change. How well does Nina know this guy? Could she have been up to no good the entire time she worked for me?

There's only a handful of customers left in the bar when the thunder roars though the small building from approaching motorcycles. Jay and I exchange looks and he heads out the door to see if this idiot has brought some more gang members here. If he has, then we'll have a problem. I'm allowing them to sit in my bar, drinking my liquor to keep the peace but to bring more members is disrespectful.

Jay walks back in and following him is Cutter and Shadow. They park their asses on a stool in front of me.

"You guys out for a ride tonight?" Cutters eyes look over to Nina and her friend.

Fuck! The last thing I need is for him is to start some shit. I need to nip this before it heads the wrong way. "If you're thinking about starting some shit take it outside. Got it?" he doesn't answer me. I finish pouring his whiskey, sliding it over to him.

Cutter slams his drink back, swallowing the contents then scoots off the stool, cracking his neck as he prepares himself for a fight. He walks over and stands in front of Nina and her man. Slowly the guy looks up, arching his neck to have to look up at Cutters imposing stature. The guy that walked in with Nina is short. He's built, but Cutter could easily stuff him under his armpit.

Words are exchanged. I don't hear much of what is said just a few words, something about the bar, Fallen Saints. When Cutter finishes speaking, I see the man's jaw tighten. He gives Nina an angry look.

So, he didn't know and Nina tricked him into coming, hoping to start shit.

The guy tilts his head at Cutter, stands up, and starts to leave but Nina grabs his forearm. Jerking his arm back he utters words to Nina. Then he disappears into the night. When a motorcycle is brought to life outside, Nina is left inside with a dazed expression on her face. When we hear his motorcycle ride off, Nina knows she's been left by herself to face us. This bitch needs to know her place.

CHAPTER 14

Maggie

Today is one of those days that you don't want to sit inside. You want to appreciate the beauty of being outside. You want the sensation of the sun warming your skin as you breathe in the crisp warm air. Plus, the view is so much better when you're outside taking in the beauty rather than looking through a windowpane. Sliding my shoes on, I slip my purse strap over my head and grab my large tote carrying my laptop, slipping it over my shoulder. I probably should text Colt but I'm only going down the street, so I decide not to bother.

When I step off in the lobby I see our doorman—Tom. He greets me as normal.

"Maggie, looking beautiful as always," he smiles, and the creases appear around his eyes. They stand out as a reminder that he had a long, happy life with his late wife.

"Thank you, Tom."

Tom has been retired from a top-notch financial company for ten years but since his wife passed away three years ago, he's been working as the doorman at my apartment building. I couldn't even imagine what he must be feeling when he goes home at night to an empty house.

Fifty years is a long time to be married. The love and memories you get to share with that person and every time you look around, all you see is their face. A time not too long ago I had hoped to find someone to share a lifetime of memories with, but now… I've given up the hope and dream of being with someone, my someone. I would settle for a boyfriend that could make it past six months.

I forget about the ache in my heart at being alone when I step outside. The cool crisp wind blows across my face, and I inhale. The end of summer is coming and I'm not looking forward to the chilly nights where I'll be wrapped up in a blanket by myself.

Get it together. I don't have to be with someone, I can enjoy life just as much by myself. No matter how many times I tell myself the same thing, I never believe it.

Pulling up the strap on my bag further, I notice a green car parked in a no-parking zone. The windows are tinted past the legal tint allowed. The car stands out against newer model cars. It could be a late seventy model. Drawing my eyes back to the sidewalk, I head toward my favorite café. I plan to indulge in the best chocolate chip cookies and drown myself in a large java chip Frappuccino while I work on my laptop in the nearby park.

Casually walking without hurrying, I take in the busy street. People are walking and talking on their phones or scrolling through social media. Cars pass by, hurrying to get to their destinations. The street I live on is always busy and I think that's one reason I love it so much.

As quick as my smile came, it leaves me replaced with an uneasiness crawling up spine, making the hairs on my neck stand up.

I scan the neighborhood, looking for anything that stands out. Walking to the park has become a norm to me, and I'm more than familiar with the streets. Nothing seems out of the ordinary, but when I turn slightly looking behind me, I spot the green sedan, the same one that was parked illegally moving at a snail's pace behind me and I know something is wrong.

They're a good two car lengths behind me, but it doesn't reassure me that they're not following me. I saw the sedan parked outside my complex and didn't give it too much thought, but now it seems like it was waiting on me all along. Maybe, just maybe, they're not following me.

Keeping my path straight, I look over my shoulder every other minute. Yep, they're still there.

My heart drops, causing the start of a panic attack to rise from the pit of my stomach. If I make any sudden movements, will they come after me? Could this be the same person who painted Whore on my car?

Overthinking leads me to pick up my pace just enough to give me a better advantage in case I need to run. I don't want it to be too obvious that I know they're behind me, so I only widen my steps. I've always had a take no shit spirit, but right now my fear is greater than my ballsy attitude and it's kicking me in the ass.

I desperately wish someone would appear out of the blue to rescue me.

The pavement under my feet becomes a blur the faster my pace keeps picking up. Pretty soon I'm running, and that's when I hear tires squeal. I scream and turn left to run down the sidewalk.

Why did I turn left?

The sidewalks are not busy on this street and if I turn back now, I'll just be running straight into the wolf's path.

Flashes of Colt come to mind. His cocky smirk, his muscular frame, and his large hands that can make me come undone. I want more. I want more than just his hands. I want to know how well he can work his body when he's inside of me, making me scream for more. I want to wrap up with him on cool nights enjoying ice cream and pizza.

The screech of tires and a car horn blaring brings me out of my lust trance. The reason is deafening when an engine roars to life behind me and I know the driver of the green sedan has come across the lane, jumping onto the sidewalk.

I run as fast as my lungs and legs let me, frantically looking for an escape. The vision of a door between two brick walls is a welcoming sight. If I can just make it there in time, I should be safe. The engine of the car comes closer, the heat of the engine burns the back of my heels as the car hits sidewalk signs, making them fly up in the air. One of the metal signs comes down with a clatter in front of me and I jump to dodge it. Just barely landing on my feet, I take off again.

Don't look back, don't look back. You can make it. Just a few more steps.

My breath is short, my bag is heavy on my shoulder, and I'm scared that my life is about to end. One step, two steps, and I'm ducking inside a doorway as the car speeds up and almost clips me as it rushes past me.

I stand in the doorway with my heart pounding, ready to burst out of my chest. Holy hell. I press my hand over my chest, taking deep breaths to calm down. I'm too scared to move, to speak, and I'm sure as hell not going to sit in a park today. I could be as dead as the day is long, sitting out in the open like a sitting duck.

My phone rings and I scream, not expecting it after the heart stopping moment I just had. My hands tremble when I open my purse. I'm barely able to push everything aside to find it. Pulling it out, I notice the number is blocked. I hesitate in answering it but end up pressing the green button.

"Hello," my voice comes choppy.

"You may have escaped this time, but you won't be the time." *Click*.

I drop my phone, hearing it bash against the concrete beside my feet. I wish I could bleed into the brick walls to fade away from this day, this moment. Why would anyone want to hurt me? Tears start to pool up and I can't help it when they roll down my cheeks and drip onto my shirt. This day had started off decent until the last twenty minutes.

My phone rings from the ground and I glance down, seeing Colt's name flash on the screen. I grab it quickly, wanting to hear his voice.

"Colt," his name comes out in a rush.

"Maggie, where are you?" his voice sounds frantic.

"I'm on Willington Street. Can you please come and get me? Someone tried to run me down and I'm too scared to leave," I sob as more tears roll down my cheeks.

"Stay on the phone. I'm headed there now. I'm leaving your apartment," I hear his footsteps thundering on the lobby floor.

"Hurry," I plead.

Keeping my body sealed up against the wall, I wait on Colt, praying that the unknown person won't try to come back. It's not long until I hear his bike turn the corner and I let out air through my mouth.

Thank you!

I run out from my hiding place and start waving my arms around, "Colt, Colt," I scream his name.

His bike comes to a stop beside me and I can't help myself as I wrap myself around his broadness, clinging to him. Wanting nothing more than to feel his body pressed up against mine. Needing to feel secure and safe, I bury my face in his neck. He says nothing, just pulls me closer. I can feel his need to be close to me vibrate through my body.

A long moment drifts by, and I don't let go until my heart has slowed and my breathing evens out.

"Thank you," I whisper.

"Hey, look at me," his hands cup my face. "Why did you leave your apartment? I told you to text me or call me."

I shrug my shoulders. It's a shitty move. I just can't talk about my stubbornness. It was stupid of me, and I won't be leaving again without letting him know.

"Climb on. I'll take you to your apartment."

I don't argue. I climb on and hold tight to his waist, laying my face up against his back. Just soaking in the feeling of being so close to him.

We walk into my apartment, and I drop my bags on the couch. Neither one of us has said a word since we left Willington Street.

CHAPTER 15

Colt

When we finished with Nina this morning, I couldn't sleep. I've never hit a woman, nor would I normally be okay with hitting one, but Nina needed to know you don't bring a rival gang member into my establishment. Her intentions were clearly to get a war started, and lucky for everyone, he was smart enough to walk away from the bar, and from Nina and her shitty ways.

The entire morning, all I wanted was to see Maggie, to tell her Jay knows she's mine. That's how I ended up at her apartment. I let myself in with the key I had made off hers. She has no idea, and doesn't know that I've strong armed one of her clients into finding someone else to start working for him next week.

Now here we stand in her living room. Maggie's mind isn't here with me. It's still back on the street where someone almost ran her over. Maggie's a strong woman, but I can tell this has more than rattled her.

I walk behind her, running my hands up her arms. Pebbles of goosebumps rise on her soft skin and her scent encases me, making me lean into her body. I know she's in a vulnerable state right now, but I can't help but wanting skin to skin contact. I want to intertwine our bodies, matching us limb to limb, and feed off the heat from the fire our bodies could start.

Maggie leans into my touch, letting her head fall back onto my chest. She's so beautiful when she gives up control. I inhale the strawberry fragrance in her hair. It must be her shampoo.

"Maggie," my voice is raspy and full of yearning.

She hums against me, "Yes," she answers my unspoken question.

Turning herself around, she wraps her arms around my neck and pulls me down till our lips almost touch. The desire I have for this woman is undeniable, but I know in my gut I need to stop this. She's just been through a traumatic event and it would be normal to want to make yourself to forget, but I don't want her to regret anything, not even a kiss. This time I want more. I want her mouth, her body, and mind. Every inch of Maggie, I want it.

"Maggie, I can't," my breath fans across her lips. "I don't want you to regret anything, not like at my dad's lake house. When I get a taste of you, there's no turning back. You're mine," I tell her honestly.

Without words, she closes the space between us, sealing our lips, and when her tongue teases mine, my body reacts, making the mint taste of her burst on my tongue. The flavor heightens with every stroke of her tongue against mine. It's a kiss that means more than just sex. It's pulling a need from me to have her planted in my life and rooted to me like I've never felt for anyone.

My hands slide down her full figure, reaching around as I grab her ass, pressing her against my dick. The need to feel more fiction is overpowering, so I thrust my hips into her. We both moan at the contact. I need more, more of her skin exposed than what I'm getting. I need her naked, the sweat from the heat of our bodies sealing us together. I reach my thumbs up, hooking them over the waistband of her yoga pants, and start tugging them down her hips. She breaks our kiss and slides her hands down my chest, yanking the hem of my t-shirt up. Then at once our hands move with feverish movements until we're both standing naked in her living room.

When I step back and look at her naked form, I inhale all the air in the room.

"Fuckkk. Maggie," I growl, rubbing my chest before I move my hand down. I want her eyes on my cock. I want her to see what she does to me.

Her eyes follow my movement and when they widen, I smirk, "Do you like what you see, pussycat?" I play with the silver ring through the head of my cock. "You want to taste it?" She nods. My voice is deep and darker than I've ever heard. "Get on your knees and I'll fuck that sassy mouth of yours."

She lowers herself to the ground without her eyes moving from my cock.

"Wait," I make her pause, grabbing a pillow off the couch as I throw it down in front of me. "Okay, on your knees. I'm ready to stick this fat cock between those fuckable lips."

She swallows.

"Go to one knee and spread your legs so I can see that pretty pussy drip for me."

She does as I ask, giving me a view of the most perfect pussy I've ever seen. Darting out her tongue, she wets her lips, getting ready to take me in.

"Don't worry, I'm about to wet them enough for you." the need to spread my cum in her mouth and on her lips has made my balls pull up high and tight, and I'm ready to unpin them. Just thinking about my cum layered over her mouth has me about to bust.

When she draws me into her mouth, a jolt of electricity shoots up my spine, "Oh fuck yes!" I hiss out. Gathering her hair into one hand, I pull it up so I can control her head. "Grab my thighs or ass to hold yourself up because I'm about to fuck that mouth hard."

She blinks her pretty blues at me, sliding her hands up to grip onto my thighs. Pushing myself into her wet mouth, I don't stop, not even when I hit the back of her throat. I press myself further down her windpipe. When her nose is firmly pressed against my stomach, I feel tingles spread through my ball sack and I know I'm almost on the verge of coming undone.

My chest is heaving and I'm having to think of anything that isn't Maggie to even out my breaths, praying that I don't come too soon, but when Maggie pulls me out and plays with my piercing with her tongue, I make the mistake of looking down watching in awe I lose it.

"Maggie, I'm…" I grit my teeth. "I'm not going to last. Hold your mouth open for me."

I grab my dick and stroke it, letting ropes of cum stream over her lips and into her mouth.

Fuckkk!

I press the tip of my cock to Maggie's lips and smear my cum over them. She surprises me when she pulls it back into her mouth and swallows. My dick jumps at the feeling. I've never felt more claimed by a woman as I do with Maggie. When I smeared myself around her lips, it was staking my claim on her, but from the moment she's sucked me back into her mouth, my body was hers and I know I won't ever be the same.

Crouching down, I wrap my arms around her and lift her into my arms. Her legs wrap around me like I was meant to fit between them.

"Where is your bathroom?" I ask as I pepper kisses along her neck.

Her breath is shallow when she speaks, "End of the hall."

I walk us into her shower and turn my back to the shower head. When the water comes on, it's chilly and it hits her in the face. Her back arches into me and

I step forward to get her out of the water till it warms up. When it does, I lower her down, letting her feet rest on the shower floor. Kissing her neck, I make my way down to her astonishing tits. Bending down, I take her nipple into my mouth and palm the other breast until I finish kissing and sucking, giving every inch of them my full attention. They're my favorite part of her body. More than a handful and the weight of their heaviness spills over my palms, making me want to do all kinds of dirty things to them.

My cock is back to rock hard, so I lift her leg up, holding it in the crock of my arm as I bend my knees, giving me the right angle I need to thrust into her. When I finally push in, her eyes squeeze closed almost as tight as her pussy is squeezing my cock.

"Baby. You're so tight," my voice breaks into a growl with my primal need to move and fuck her hard against the shower wall, but I want to make sure she knows this is more than just a quick fuck. "Open your eyes and look at me. I want you to see all the emotions I feel when I'm inside of you."

Our eyes connect. There's so much care that shines through hers it's almost overwhelming. Maggie is a deep person. Someone that cares about the people who are around her and I want to be a permanent fixture in those eyes. I want her to see me for the man that would do anything to care for her, provide for her, and to protect her with my life.

Brushing my lips against hers, I move slowly, wanting her to feel how much she means to me and how badly I want this connection to last. A few slow strokes and I pick up my pace.

"I need you."

Her nails dig into my shoulders and it's my undoing. Holding her legs up, I fuck her against the shower wall. When she screams and closes her eyes, I growl. I want them on me.

"Open your eyes," I demand.

With her pussy squeezing me and the lust haze in her eyes, I follow suit, unloading myself in her wet heat, not allowing myself to blink. I keep my eyes locked on hers. I'm too lost in the heavens as I stare into the blissfulness of her gaze.

We finish washing each other, taking our time, and I use it to memorize every curve, dip, and inch as I glide the soapy washcloth over every naked inch of her body.

"Do you want to lay on the couch and watch a movie? Or we could lay in the bed till something rises," angling my eyes at my cock, I raise an eyebrow.

"I need to work today," her words are a little shy, and I wonder if I have pushed her into something too soon.

"I'm not leaving," I whisper softly, sliding my hands up the sides of her body, enjoying the feel of her soft skin. I skim the sides of her full-sized breasts, over her collarbones and cupping her cheeks. "I won't bother you, but I'm not leaving you. What happened today shouldn't have happened," I shake my head, trying to throw the thought of what could have been out of my mind. "If I was here—"

"Don't..." her words come out quick. "It could as easily happen if you were there," her hands rest against mine on her cheeks and I lower my forehead to meet hers.

"Let's get out, the water is turning cold," reaching over, I turn the water off and grab her a towel.

Once we are dried off and she puts on a long shirt, I take it from her, "I want you naked today."

"Colt!" her voice comes out like she's surprised. "I'm not walking around you naked all day."

"Why not? It's not like I haven't been standing in the shower for the last two hours looking at this beautiful body?" I reply, using my hand I make a swiping motion down her body.

Her checks turn a rosy color, and I can smell the wheels burning in her mind, thinking about walking around naked all day in front of me.

"Fine, but Do. Not. Disturb me. I really do need to work," she walks out in her birthday suit, and I smile at her peach ass walking away.

Maggie sits at a small desk in her living room. It's close to the patio doors that face the couch where I'm spread out, laying lazily, pretending to watch something on the tube. I switch my eyes back and forth from the television and stealing glances at Maggie. I could sit here all day and stare at this view.

I rise up on my side and reach down to stroke myself. Sitting here watching Maggie has made me hard and since I said I wouldn't bother her, I decide to help myself with the problem. Maggie's legs are open, giving me the prefect view of her slick mound. I have a sneaking suspicion she's doing that on purpose.

My phone rings on the floor where my pants were dropped to. I know that ringtone. It's my dad's. Maggie looks up from her laptop with a blush warming her cheeks.

Yep, totally on purpose.

"Hey dad," I say, greeting him with ease.

"Colt," Connie's voice comes through the line, making a slight tremor erupt in my back. Pulling the phone back, I recheck the screen, verifying its dads and not Connie's phone.

I sit up in a hurry, "Connie, why are you calling from dad's phone? Is something wrong?" Alarms go off in my head. She wouldn't be calling if something wasn't wrong. Jumping to my feet, I walk into Maggie's small kitchen, suddenly needing more space to breathe.

"Your dad is okay right now, but he's in the hospital," and just like that, I feel my soul float out of body.

CHAPTER 16

Colt

"Mom," I yell out when I walk into my parents' bedroom. "Mom, where are you?" my voice carries through the large room as I walk to the open bathroom door.

My dad has been working from home for the past month, but today he said he had to go in for a meeting that he couldn't get out of. He told me to look after mom, to make sure she was resting and to take care of the house.

Our house has always had a warm and inviting feeling for all our friends and family, but since my mom has been sick, it's been empty and cold. Her smile doesn't warm up the house like it used to. Sometimes she tries to get out of bed, but she doesn't make it too far before her strength gives out. Leaving her with no choice but to go back to bed.

Stepping around the door frame, I gasp when I see my mom laying on the hard marble floor. Running over to her, I try to shake her, hoping she'll open her eyes, but she doesn't. Her body doesn't budge even with me roughly nudging her to move. She lays still. Under her nose looks like dried blood that has dripped to the floor. The sight of her laying lifeless causing a panic in my heart. I feel helpless and alone.

Please, please, wake up. I beg silently.

My vision blurs as I run to the telephone in my parents' bedroom, dialing my dad's cell phone number as quickly as my fingers allow me. When he answers, I get a small glimpse of hope, he'll know what I need to do to help my mom.

"Dad, something is wrong with momma. She's laying on the bathroom floor and won't wake up. What do I do?" my voice is scratchy and tears stream down my face.

"I'm coming," he hangs up before answering my question.

I do the only thing I can. I cry. I cry for the loss in my heart, for the mother that I once knew to be the strongest person in my life. The life that is passing before my eyes. The life that's being cut down, for the person who hasn't had enough time to offer the world all of her beauty.

My chest is heavy, and my eyesight is a blur. I hear Maggie's voice, but it's like I'm in a tunnel, fighting to crawl my way out. There's nothing but blackness and Maggie's voice is the light. It's drawing me out of the darkness bit by bit.

"Colt. Colt," Maggie's voice calls to me. It gives me the strength to keep searching until I can see her.

My voice is a whisper, "Maggie."

"I'm here. I'm right here. You're okay."

My vision becomes clear. The sight of Maggie's angelic face comes into view, and it causes the heaviness in my chest to ease off just knowing she's here with me. It's a feeling that I want to wake up to every morning.

I have the same dream every year around this time. The anniversary of my mother's death is creeping up like a shadow of guilt. It's the guilt of living and how she doesn't get to. She was taken away at a young age, much younger than she should have been.

"Can you sit up?" she asks, her expression is laced with concern.

I nod. Sitting up, I rub the back of my head. I must have hit it pretty hard when I fell onto the kitchen floor. Twisting my body around, I look for my phone but don't see it. Maggie must read my mind because she hands it to me.

"When you fell, I ran over. Your step-mom was yelling, so..." she drifts off when she speaks. "I answered it. I hope you don't mind," she blinks, waiting for me to respond.

Remembering what Connie said, it makes my mouth run dry. I try to swallow, but there's nothing to swallow back.

"I didn't even ask what hospital they were at," I still feel light-headed from hearing Connie say my dad was in the hospital.

"Don't worry. I got all the information. If you feel like going, I'll drive us there."

Maggie helps me get to my feet. I do my best not to put all my weight on her. I'm much heavier than she is, and I don't want to hurt her.

Her warm touch around my waist is welcome. It sends a warmth through me, knowing she is here by my side. The last time I was alone to deal with a traumatic experience, I lost myself in my head. The thought of doing it again gives me an uneasy wave of numbness, shivering though me.

"Thank you," wrapping my arms around her, I pull her to me, kissing her forehead. "I'm ready."

CHAPTER 17

Maggie

When Colt falls in my kitchen, landing on the floor with a loud thud, my voice elevates to a pitch that I don't recognize as my own voice when I scream out his name. I leap up to run to his side. This strong bulky man that handles everything with a calmness crumbles to my floor. My tears burn behind my eyes as the pain from an arrow pierces my heart. The intense blank look on his face is a state of disorientation. A tear drops from the corner of his normally bright eyes. I don't think he's even able to comprehend he let it escape.

A woman's voice echoes from the floor. Picking up his phone, I speak with uncertainty. Dread scales up my backbone of what I'm about to hear. The woman's voice gets louder, calling out for Colt.

"Hello," the sound of my voice is shaky and unsure of who Colt was talking to.

"Who is this?" a voice that I recognize makes me hunch my shoulders up past my ears.

Fuck!

Colt's witchy witch stepmother's voice is like nails firing off into my head. I hate that he's related to her, even if only through marriage. They didn't seem close when I was at their lake house over the summer. I gather my strength and close my eyes because I'm not going anywhere. I won't let her decide if I will or won't date Colt. I won't let anyone decide for me. She should be happy now that I'm not dating Charles, her precious child. He's a thirty-two-year-old man that still runs to his mama whenever he needs his wounds licked.

"Maggie," I answer, determined that she can take it or shove it. This is not the time to be petty. Something is definitely wrong if Colt fell to the floor the way he did.

I hear her scoff in the background, and I immediately want to backhand her.

"Connie, is something wrong with Connor? Colt's face is void and I'm worried," lucky for her she doesn't say something she'll regret later. I'm in no mood for her bullshit.

"Connor is in the hospital at Carraway. The doctors said he will be fine, but they are keeping him overnight, maybe two nights. I'm not sure yet."

"We're on our way," I hang up before she can comment. I know where Carraway is. My grandmother's physician's office was there, and I used to take her for visits when I was a senior in high school.

"Colt," tapping his face, I call out again to him. "Colt."

His voice is barely audible. He mutters my name, but I'm still not sure if he's fully aware of his surroundings. I couldn't even imagine how he's feeling. If it was one of my parents, I would be losing my shit. My parents are pillars in my life, always holding me up and supporting me even when I screw up. Everyone deserves a support team like them. I never take a moment for granted, never forget to let them know they're the reason I've worked so hard for what I have.

"I'm here. I'm right here. You're okay," my pulse picks up. I have no experience being someone's support. Now is the time to put what my family's done for me to use for thinking about what I need to do for him. "Can you sit up?"

He blinks his eyes, pushing himself up. His gaze sweeping around him on the floor. I know he's looking for his phone, that in my hand. I reach out to give it to him. He doesn't hesitate to take it.

"When you fell, I ran over and your step-mom was yelling so..." I drift off. "I answered it. I hope you don't mind," my nerves are kicking in, waiting for him to answer.

Please don't be upset.

Charles used to hate it when I would answer his phone. I only answered because he was in the shower or was asleep. You never know when an emergency could come up and you need someone to get the message to you as quickly as possible. He used to scream at me not to answer his phone under any circumstance. I know why he didn't want me to answer it now. Most men don't cheat just once they do it until they get caught. Some men don't even stop then, like my cousin Jennifer's husband did. Poor thing.

"I didn't even ask what hospital they were at," he sounds so defeated.

"Don't worry. I got all the information. If you feel like going, I'll drive you there."

"Thank you," he says, wrapping his arms around me. He pulls me in and kisses my forehead. "I'm ready."

The entire ride over, Colt hasn't said a word. I've stolen glances at him, hoping he would look my way, but he doesn't seem to acknowledge anything. I can't fault him for it. I would be lost in my head and not wanting to speak to anyone if I were in his shoes. It doesn't satisfy my need to want to hug and comfort him, but I need to respect his space.

It doesn't take long to arrive at the hospital. It's almost outside the city limits. Carraway is a little older than most of the other hospitals. It's mainly where the older generation to come, while the younger generations use the more high-tech hospitals. I'm surprised Connie brought Connor here. She doesn't seem the kind of person who would step foot into anything that wasn't more than top-notch.

The elevator stops at the fifth floor.

"Do you want me to wait in the waiting room?" I ask, secretly hoping he'll say yes. I still feel a little weird about seeing his parents after being at their house with their other son.

"No, go in with me," he extends his hand and I meet it, letting his envelope mine.

The way his fingers lace with mine leaves me wanting this connection between us to never end. His hands are large, with scars covering his knuckles. Being an owner of a bar, he must get into a lot of fights. I picture a pissed off Colt slamming some jerk into the floor and bashing their head in. It has an effect on my body, sending electric tingles to my core.

Connors' room is near the nurse's station and with the door open, I can see Connie's side profile. I shouldn't be as nervous as I am, but there's something about Connie that makes my skin want to crawl right off my bones. I can't imagine her as a loving mother to Colt. She seems far more interested in keeping her own grown son, Charles, in baby mode for the rest of his life. Whereas Colt is very much a man, I imagine that's all because of his father. It makes me wonder what kind of genuine relationship Connor and Connie have. Do they love each other the way couples should, or is it for show? But if I think about it, I didn't really see them looking cozy with each other the entire time I was at their lake house.

"Colt," Connor's voice booms from his bed, where

he lies with a smile reaching from ear to ear.

Connor has to be in his mid to late forties. The man is still in good shape. His arms are full of muscles and his long legs look like they are bent in the bed that is clearly too small for him. My eyes scan the rest of him and it's very hard not to miss the large package that only a thin grown and a sheet are laying on top of. I can see it's a family trait to have large packages, and I give thanks for it. I give thanks even more because Colt knows exactly what to do with it.

"Dad," Colt's voice seems to have less tension than it did when we first arrived. "I'm glad to see you looking well." He walks over to Connor's bedside with me still in tow, giving him a hug with his free arm. "You remember Maggie?"

Connor smiles even bigger making me feel less out of place.

"Maggie, good to see you again. I hope my son is treating you well?" his eyebrow lifts when he looks at Colt.

Yeah, I know. Done with one son, move on to the next.

"Yes sir," I swallow, not sure on what else to say.

Connie coughs from her seat on the other side of Connor's bed. For a brief moment, we forgot she was here. *Damn, too bad she's not.*

Colt's eyes search the room, "Where's Charles?" his question surprises me. I shouldn't expect him not to ask. Charles is his stepbrother. I'm just surprised he would expect him to be here. Charles is a selfish ass that only thinks of himself.

"He's busy," Connie fires back.

I internally roll my eyes. I can't see him being so busy that he couldn't be here for the man that supported him and his mother. Unless he's struck up his bosses' ass trying to climb the corporate ladder. Which is what he's wanted from the day I met him.

"Don't you think he should be here?" Colt's voice is stern.

His gaze holds Connie's, giving her a look that should have bursting up in ashes.

"Colt," Connor snaps. "He's busy. Leave it," Connor's voice sounds tried.

He drops my hand and blows out air, letting the steam release out his nostrils.

"Sorry Dad. Tell me what the doctor said," Colt grabs a seat, pulling it to his dad's side and pats his leg for me to sit.

"Why don't we head out and give them some room to talk," Connie comments with her overly sickening sweet voice.

"Colt, do you want me to stay?" I ask, silently pleading for him to say yes.

"It's okay, go ahead and grab a drink," he pulls his wallet out, handing me a couple of dollars. It wasn't necessary, but I did appreciate the thought of him taking care of me.

Connie and I follow the signs pointing down the hallway to a small waiting area with some vending machines in it. There's only silence between us. I'm so relieved she's as eager to speak to me as I am with her but when we step inside the waiting room and the door shuts a switch is flipped. Connie's alter ego comes out in swinging mode. Gripping my bicep with her claws letting them dig into my arm. I want to wince but I don't. I don't want her to see she gets to me in anyway.

"If one doesn't work then you just move to the next," her statement doesn't hurt anywhere near as much as her nails digging into my skin. "Who's next? Connor?" she raises her eyebrows.

What a bitch!

Doing my best to stay calm, I jerk my arm out of her boney hand. I choose to ignore her questioning me and walk over to the vending machine, staring at it. I don't care about getting a drink, I just wanted to move out of her grip. She doesn't give up because I can feel her standing beside me. Bringing herself in my personal space, her mouth comes to my ear, whispering anything but sweet thoughts.

"You're the reason why my son is having a nervous breakdown," her words almost make me bark out a laugh. Whipping my head so fast to look her in the eye, it makes her take a step back. Good.

"If anyone is making your precious boy lose his ever-loving mind that would be you. You nurse him like an infant. I've never seen a grown man act like such a baby around his mother the way he does around you. If you would let the boy come up for air every so often instead of on your saggy tit he might grow up," I storm out of the room.

Anger pumps through my body as I stomp down the hallway. That bitch must be in denial if she thinks I'll stand there and let her degrade me more. She clearly cannot see she's the reason why Charles has a hard time coping with being told no. What the hell did she mean he's having a nervous breakdown? I've only seen Charles once in months and he looked disheveled, but never would I have thought Charles would be on the edge of a mental breakdown. He's always been put together.

I blow air out between my lips. Right now, I need to burn some energy, so I keep walking around hoping I'll get it in check before I go back to Colt. I don't know if I should tell him or let it slide how his stepmother talked to me. I decide for right now that I should go with the latter, since he's having to deal with his father's health. I just hope she doesn't open her freaking mouth and spill lies about me to Colt. She could say I goaded her into an argument, or worse. She might add that I was asking about Charles, and how I might still have feelings for him. That woman seems like the kind of person that would do anything to get what she wanted.

CHAPTER 18

Colt

The smell of death and sadness floods my mind when I enter the lobby. I haven't been in a hospital in over thirteen years. I shake myself, wanting and needing the memories of my mother's demise to fall away. Wonderful memories should outweigh those last moments, but they don't. They keep in the front, blocking out her smile and how she lit up the room when she entered. She made every day the best with her beauty.

Dad crouches down beside momma, then three men dressed in white shirts and blue pants hurry in behind him, with two of them pushing a small metal bed. When Dad wraps his arms around me, it's to pull me back to get me out of their way. The men start pulling out what looks like metal flat irons and wires. They quickly put stickers on her chest, attaching a wire to one of them.

I don't know what they are doing. A small amount of gel

is put on the irons and the man rubs the irons together. He yells clear, and he presses the irons to momma's chest. A sound pierces my ears, then momma's chest jumps. It makes her body jump up off the floor, then back down. They do it again, making more tears flow down my cheeks. I want to tell them to stop. She doesn't need to be hurt like that. She's much too fragile, so small, and I want to wrap myself around her, shielding her from everyone.

A beeping noise picks comes up on the small machine as a steady beat. Immediately, they drop the equipment and put more stickers on her, connecting wires to the stickers. Everything around us is loud, and the chaos is too much, making my heart pound and my mind roll in a whirlwind. Everything spins around me, and I can't even feel. I don't feel dad's arms around me, holding me like he's trying to keep me from running. All I can see is my mom being lifted on the stretcher. My breath comes out in short, quick puffs. I can't lose her. Who will make my lunch? Who will dance with me in the kitchen? I'm too young to lose her. Breathe in, breathe out.

The bed rises and clicks into place with a thump, making her arm fall from her side. I reach out, brushing our fingers together. I look up to dad and see his eyes filled with grief.

No words are exchanged as we follow the ambulance. Cars are pulling over as the red lights flash and the siren rings out in front of us. I swallow back the questions I want to ask, but don't dare to say out loud. Dad's barely able to keep himself together. His lips tremble, and I know he's trying to hide it from me, but I see it when he doesn't think I can.

We walk into a lobby where people are sitting around in bandages. Their heads are wrapped and a smell in the air crawls up my nose. I sniff, trying to figure out what it is. Coughing on the stench. I realize it's the stench of death.

"Dad, where's momma?" I ask with a quiver in my voice. My heart is beating faster than it ever has, but I know it's strong. Momma tells me all the time how strong I am. She's always my biggest fan at my soccer games. Cheering me on when I do well and when I don't, she's the first to say encouraging words like to shake it off that everyone has an off day.

Dad doesn't answer my question, he's too busy talking to a lady at the front desk. I stand and wait for him to tell me where she is but I never get my answer because a man in a white coat comes out and directs us to a small room that has four chairs in it. The facial expression on my dad's face is crushing. He looks so lost. I'm confused what is going on until the man in the white coat says something that makes my heart feel weak.

I guess I'm not as strong as momma said I was, because I put my face into my hands and cry. When I hear sobs louder than mine, I know my dad is devastated and I pull myself out of my hands to wrap my short arms around him, trying to make sure he knows I'm still here. That it may be just us, but I'm still here for him.

The elevator stops at the fifth floor bringing me out of my past.

Maggie asks if I would like for her to wait in the waiting room. I know I can't do this without her. I need her to be by my side. No one has told me what is going on with my dad, and for all I know, it could be cancer. Losing one parent to that horrible disease was enough for a lifetime, but if I have to do with it with my father, I just didn't know how strong I can be.

It doesn't take us long to find dad's room and when he calls out my name; I let some of the tension release from my shoulders. He looks better than I expected, even if his color is slightly pale. Sitting up in his bed, his smile gives me hope that it's nothing too serious.

Connie is sitting by his bed with the appearance of a grieving widow. Grieving would be an understatement if she was to lose his paycheck. She'd more than likely lose her damn mind if she lost my father's income. Connie never has been hateful to my dad. She's more than cared for him and I know their relationship never seemed to have cracks, but there were missing parts to their marriage. The intimate ways of hugging, kissing, and touching each other weren't there, not like the way my dad was with my mom. He could never keep his hands off her, and it would always embarrass me when we were out or when my friends were over at our house. Their marriage seemed more of a business arrangement.

Connie was more of a stand in, someone to help raise me. I think Dad just stuck around after I grew up because he felt he owed her something. He thinks she helped get me through those rough teenage years. Little does he know she only made it worse. Her style of motherhood was punishing more than caring when it came to me. Always showering her son, Charles with the affection that I once had with my own mother in front of my eyes while she barely fed me crumbs on care. The crumbs she threw at me were only in front of my dad, which made me despise her more.

"You remember Maggie?" Dad smiles and tells her it's good to see her again. He turns to me and winks.

Yeah, I know dad I saw her in that bikini, remember.

That damn small leather bikini, I can't seem to get the image of out of my head. Dad's eyes almost fell out of his head when he saw how her body was made to wear something so small. I can still remember what he said when we were alone about Charles not being able to handle a woman like her. He's never been someone to make comments about another woman but Maggie isn't an ordinary woman. She's special and I plan on holding onto her with all the strength I have.

A few pleasant words are exchanged before Connie and Maggie give us some space to talk. I'm thankful for Connie leaving. I wanted to ask dad a few questions alone, without her being around.

Once they leave the room and are far enough down the hall, I get up and close the door. Something changes in his appearance, and I can tell he's more tried than he's letting on.

"Are you going to tell me why you're in the hospital?"

He lays his head back, using the remote to lower the head of the bed.

"Food poisoning."

I scrunch up my nose, "Where did you eat at?"

"Home," his declaration confuses me.

"I thought your housekeeper emptied all the refrigerators and freezers every month. Is Missy not working for you anymore?"

He shakes his head, "Not since the end of last month."

Have things gotten that bad with money?

"I know what you're thinking and it's not that," he avoids looking at me when he says it.

"Then tell me," my voice rises. "What is it?" when he says nothing I add on to my questions. Lowering my voice, I ask, "Why is Connie here? I thought you were getting a divorce."

He closes his eyes and exhales, "She came by the house to get a few things and thankfully she did, or I would still be laying on the floor," he hesitates. "We've been talking, trying to sort things out. We're going to give it another shot. She's promised to get a job and sell stuff to pay off her debts."

I shake my head, knowing this is another one of Connie's mind games. She won't be happy until she has drained my father completely dry. I don't say as much, but getting a job has never been an interest she has expressed. What would she say to her country club friend's if she had to get a job? She would rather die than be talked about among the rich and spoiled.

"Dad. Are you sure this is what you want? I can't help but feel like…"

Connie opens the door and walks into the room. I

don't bother finishing what I was going to say. There's no point. Connie's got her claws into dad, and I don't even think he's aware of it. I decide to drop it for now. Hopefully, he'll come to his senses, and it won't be too late for him to give her the boot.

Maggie doesn't follow Connie in.

"Where's Maggie?" I ask Connie.

"She… had to stop off at the ladies' room," Connie says with a dark cloud brewing in her eyes.

Hmm, I look at her, but she doesn't keep eye contact with me, instead she glances over to look at the monitors that are keeping dad's heart rate. She's lying. I can see her eyes are telling a different story. A story that I'm going to find out about from Maggie.

Connie doesn't bother sitting down beside dad on the bed, instead she sits in a large chair across the room with her perfect posture. A steel rod in her spine, and her manicured nails that looks fresh, she oozes narcissism.

There's silence filling the room, none of us speak and since Maggie's not back, I'm growing concerned.

"I'm going to go find Maggie. She should have been here by now," I look at Connie when I say it. I want her to know I don't really buy her story.

She doesn't speak or acknowledge I'm going to find her, instead she looks down at her overpriced nails that look way too much like claws.

When I leave the room, I walk by the glass windows that peer in the waiting room that's empty. I bypass the nurses' station when a young woman dressed in scrubs bumps into me.

"Sorry, I wasn't looking," she blushes.

"No problem," she walks away. "Excuse me," I touch her shoulder lightly. "Have you seen a woman that's has blonde hair. She's wearing black yoga pants and an off shoulder long pink top?" It may be a bit of a stretch that the nurse has seen her, but I need to know where Maggie is.

"Yes, there's a small area," she points down the hallway. "To the left for seating. I just got back from my break and she's in there."

"Thank you," I take off, hoping Maggie's there.

When I turn the corner, I see Maggie sitting with her legs crossed, head tilted back, and eyes closed. She's inhaling and exhaling in deep breaths, looking pissed off. Connie had to have said something. Taking the seat next to her, I rest my hand on her thigh. She jumps and I chuckle at her. I shouldn't, but she looks so damn cute. My little fierce pussycat.

"I didn't mean to scare my pussy… cat," she's a vision of sex appeal. That one shoulder top makes me want to lick her collarbone and suck my way down to those perfect tits.

"I was in deep thought," she huffs.

"Really, was it about my cock inside that tight cunt of yours?"

She rolls her eyes closed. I know she's thinking about us fucking earlier. I'm already hard just thinking about it myself.

Holding her hand, I place it on my rock hard cock

that's needing her softness to hold it. She tries to jerk away, looking to see if someone will see us, but I don't let her.

"Unzip my pants or I'll do it, but I need your hands on my cock." It's not a question or a request. I need the skin-on-skin connection and since we can't get naked. I'll take a hand or blow job right now.

"Colt," her eyes dart back to the small open doorway. "Somebody is going to see us," she tries to pull her hand away again, but I hold it firmly against my dick and start to guide it up and down my shaft.

"Pussycat, they can watch you suck me off for all I care. As long as they don't see that body that's mine, I don't care."

"If you're going to be mine, then I don't want anyone seeing that big ass dick of yours," she comments with a bite to her words, and it makes me smile like a fool.

"Fuck!" I slam our lips together, tasting her, savoring it. Fuck, she tastes like... Mine.

CHAPTER 19

Maggie

I smooth my hair down looking in the visor mirror. Before we went and told Connor and Connie we were leaving, we stepped in an accessible restroom. Colt had me pinned up against the wall as soon as the door shut, and he clicked the lock. I've never had a lover like him. He's packing and can use it. I never would have guessed that he's as responsible as he is. He's got me feeling all kind of things, and I just hope I'm not disappointed, but there is still the age thing. I can't seem to get completely passed it.

"What are you in deep thought over there about?" Colt asks.

Not wanting to talk about my thoughts, I ask him a question, "Your dad looked good. Did he say why they brought him in? Does it have anything to do with his heart?" I ask, worried that he may have had a heart attack.

He narrows his eyes at me, but I don't flinch. Changing the subject was too obvious, I should have been more subtle about it.

"Are you hiding something?" he pulls the car over to the shoulder and parks it.

Turning his big beautiful body to me, he snakes his hand behind my head, pulling me into his personal space, "I have ways to make you talk," he says seductively.

Brushing his lips against mine his tongue slides out and licks my bottom lip. I moan.

Fuck me! He's good.

If he only knew how dry of a sex life I've had, I wonder if he would make a vow to make it up to me?

Oh God Maggie, he's more than just a cock. A big, smooth, thick, hard as hell dick that could drive nails into the thickest wood that exist.

"Are you going to tell me, or do I need to take action?"

"I don't know about this age gap between us," I blurt out.

Sitting back in the driver's seat, he blinks, "Really, is that it?" he says like it's not a big deal.

"Yes. Did you think it was something else?"

"I was thinking Connie said or did something to you when you left dad's room," he says as he pulls back on the interstate.

A shiver runs up my back. Connie gives me a vibe of being evil.

"She's not the nicest person to be around, but I

think the reason she's like that to me is because of Charles. It doesn't have to do with you," Colt picks up speed, gripping the steering wheel with a little more force now.

"Colt, you might want to slow down," grabbing the oh shit handle, I hold on. "Colt!" I scream his name when he dodges from hitting the back of a car.

"Sorry," he shakes his head, visibly trying to relax. "My dad... well... I thought he was going to divorce her," he stalls trying to tell me.

"I couldn't blame him if he did," I mutter to myself. "Why would you think that? Did he tell you?"

"Sort of. We talked just recently, and I think she just slid herself back into his life," he sounds bitter over it.

I wonder just how good of a step-mom she was to him. Baby steps. Baby steps. I don't want to come across as a nosey bitch. Not that I'm not. I just don't want Colt thinking that way of me until he really gets to know me.

"About the age thing," he raises his eyebrows, looking at me from the corner of his eye.

Fuck! He's handsome.

"I think my cock tells you a different story. Don't you? I'm more than of age and the right size."

I laugh, "Yeah, well, you're right about that. I just have had this thing where I've only dated men that are older than me."

"Maggie," he reaches for my hand, interlacing our fingers. "I'm not worried about the small difference of our age, and I don't think you should be either. I can and will take care of you because whether you like it or not, you're not getting rid of me. I'm here to stay."

I've never had a man that wanted to be with me for me. They usually end up running, screaming in the path that leads them the furthest from me. This man screams bad ass. The kind of bad ass that will fuck you up. A savage protector. My heart does a flip.

I squeeze his hand.

"Take me home and fuck me like the beast you are," I smile, but I'm fucking serious.

***

"I rode my bike here, but I'll follow you in your car to work." Colt announces.

He's drying off after the ultimate sex-a-thon we just had. Four orgasms and a shower later, my body is like a limp noodle. I've never been so completely sexually satisfied. I'm going to have to divorce my vibrator. I don't see a future for him anymore. Colt has set the bar high, and I know if he changes his mind and doesn't want to be with me, I'll have to upgrade to something much larger than what's in my nightstand. Which still wouldn't compare to him. I'm falling for him faster than I would like to admit.

We both just got out of the shower and I'm sitting on the edge of the bed, watching him get dressed in awe. I enjoy having him in my space. Watching him make himself at home gives me a warm feeling coursing through me. Could Colt be it?

A cell rings in the living room, and I know it's not

my ring tone, "That's your phone, do you want me to get it for you?" I ask Colt as he continues to shave. I openly stare at his muscles and abs. Each smooth stroke he makes shaving outlines the contour of them.

"If you don't mind," Colt replies as he runs the razor up his throat. I gave him one of the extra razors I keep on hand.

I dodge out of the bedroom, hair still dripping, and grab his phone from the end table. The name Sabrina is lighting up on the screen.

"Who is it?" Colt asks, yelling from the bathroom.

He wouldn't? Would he? No. I don't think he's a two timer, but he's in a bike gang. They do like to play around on their women, don't they? Don't let it be true, please. Don't let me be another fool falling for someone that only wants a side piece, or that tells me I'm not good enough for them.

I must have stood looking at the screen for too long, because Colt takes the phone out of my hand.

"It's not what you think," he rejects the call, sending it to his voicemail.

He cups my face, tilting it upwards to meet his eyes, "She used to be someone I hooked up with but since I met you, I haven't been with anyone. There's no one who compares to you," he looks genuine saying it, and I want desperately to believe him. "Say something," his words fan across my forehead as he places a gentle kiss on my kiss.

"I..." my brain is too foggy. His sweet words have always been something that I've wanted to hear, and knowing they come from his lips make them sweeter. "I feel the same way," I confess. "Except for that one date I had," the words tumble out like vomit. "Oh my goodness, was it bad? But I couldn't think about being with anyone because you're the only one I could think about."

It is the honest truth. I've thought about him the entire time, not just the way he finger fucked me on the float, but the way he made me feel. How he took the time to care for me when he busted my nose with the volleyball. Spiking the ball toward me to get my attention, but what he didn't know was that my eyes were on him the entire time. I even caught Nat taking glances at him that made me want to scratch her eyes out.

"Are you going to call her back?" I ask with insecurity. Did she mean anything to him? I need to make sure before I give him anymore of my heart.

His hands still cupping my face and his eyes boring into mine, he says, "Not a chance. She meant nothing to me. I never wanted to wake up with my arms wrapped around her or even take her out on a proper date like we're doing tonight," my eyes light up.

"I thought we were going to work."

He shakes his head, "Nope. I've got a big night planned. A surprise for you. I hope you like seafood."

Excitement fills me making me giddy, "I love seafood!" I tell him honestly.

"Good, because you're going to need your energy. I

plan on fucking you six ways to Sunday tonight," he says, sending a rush of heat to my core.

CHAPTER 20

Colt

The Gulfs Surf is one of the best seafood restaurants in North Carolina, and it happens to be my favorite. Maggie and I sit at a table on the patio with the sounds of crashing waves surrounding us. Other than the strings of light along the deck, there's a view of complete darkness as far as we can see. The wind picks up, blowing off the ocean, making Maggie's hair whirl around her. She looks like a golden goddess.

"It's beautiful here," she smiles, looking out in the endless body of water. The faint lights of boats drift by in the distance reminding us of our spectacular view covered by the midnight air.

I stare at the beauty in front of me, "It's something to behold for sure," my voice is breathy.

The sundress she's wearing hugs her chest and I can tell she's not wearing a bra underneath because her nipples are like hard peaks peeping through the thin material. Every time the wind blows, they become more pronounced. It's not helping the situation in my pants. My dick is trying to break free with every glimpse I take. I want nothing more than to wrap my teeth around them and flick them with my tongue.

The wind picks up, and she closes her eyes and slightly parts her mouth, enjoying the cool breeze on her face. I can't stop myself when I lean over the table to steal a kiss. When I pull back, I'm drawn in by the sight of her blue eyes. She smiles, and it makes me only hungrier for her.

"Hmm, I can't help but want to taste your lips when you look like that."

She blinks like she's not understanding what I'm saying, "How did I look?"

I let out a heavy breath, "You look like you do when you come," she swallows.

Someone clears their throat, breaking the heated moment between us. Our server doesn't make eye contact with either of us. While the waitress pretends to be writing something down, Maggie's eyes are cast down, embarrassment coursing through her. I shake my head, grinning. I don't care who hears me. Maggie had that look of total bliss on her face, right before she screams that she's about to come. It's the sexist sight I've ever seen, and I plan on making her scream out my name more.

I place our order, telling the server we'll have the seafood platter, pairing it with a bottle of Cabernet

Sauvignon. The platter is large enough to feed a table of four and comes with a variety of seafood along with sides. Since this is her first time here, it'll give her more to taste than just one dish but I'm more than happy to get her another dish if she likes.

Maggie stares at me when I place the order for us and I'm hoping she's not offended I ordered for her.

"Was that okay?" she pinches her eyebrows together. "Ordering for you. I just thought since you've never been here, I could order the sampler since it'll have different options on it."

She smiles making me relax that she's not upset.

"Yes, it sounded really good. I didn't know what to order. Everything sounds so good. Maybe, the next time I come, I will know what to order."

"I hope you're planning on coming on me later," I wink.

"Sir," the waitress says, looking five shades of red. "I'll need to see some I.D.," the waitress informs me.

Maggie snickers at the waitress carding me. I'll have to remember to punish her for having fun at my expense. Which really will be more of an enjoyment than a punishment, at least for me.

I pull out my wallet and show her my driver's license. She nods and lets us know she'll be back with the wine.

"What was so funny?" I ask seriously. I'm teasing Maggie under the table, playfully pushing her feet apart.

Her jaw drops, whispering, "What are you

doing?" she tries to move her feet between mine to close her legs, but I keep mine firmly on the floor.

The table is not very wide between us, and my legs are long enough to enclose hers between them or vice versa.

"I have a dress on," she looks around, trying to catch anyone that might be looking at us.

"Don't worry," I coax her. "Have you ever been fucked on the beach? We can take a walk after dinner," her eyes bob around and I can see the splotches on her face from the soft lighting enclosed around us.

"Colt," she fidgets with the silverware. "I'm not having this conservation right here," she whispers. I bet she's never had sex in a public place. A thrill runs through me, making me want to claim that first experience.

"Maggie," I whisper her name, coming closer to her over the table. "Have you ever had sex outside of the bedroom?"

A shadow stands at my side. Thinking it must be the waitress, I rest back into my seat, hoping she'll put our food down and disappear. But when two more enormous shadows appear, I cringe.

It's not only my favorite spot to eat, but it's also several of my brothers' favorite. I just didn't think it through when I wanted to bring Maggie here. Bringing her here was my way of giving another piece of me to her.

Staring up at the three shit eating grins assholes beside me, Cutter, J-Bird are giving Maggie the biggest fuck me eyes. While Shadow looks more reserve as always. He's the most dangerous out of everyone, but he's also the quietest out of all the guys. What they say is true. It's always the quiet ones you have to watch out for.

"Look boys. If it isn't my favorite brother," Cutter laughs, patting me hard on the shoulder.

"Go away fuckhead, I'm busy."

"Who is this beautiful lady?" Cutter asks, picking up Maggie's hand and kissing it.

What the fuck! He's anything but a gentleman.

I push my chair back, letting it scrap the floor, "Let go of her," I growl out.

Cutter cuts me a grin and Shadow puts his hand on his shoulder, "Stop fucking around or you're about to get your ass handed to you," Shadow tells Cutter.

"Fuck man," he looks back to Maggie. "I'm only playing, sweetheart. You look like you're ready to run. He's an ass," he points his thumb at me. "If he gives you shit, you come find me. I can take care of you," I leap up into action, but J-Bird and Shadow hold me back.

Hands in the air, Cutter grins, "I'm only messing with you, calm down fucker," he winks walking away. "Come on, boys. Let's go to the bar."

Cutter is always fucking around with me when it comes to women. He's got a few years in age over me, but he never misses an opportunity to give me shit, teasing me that I don't know how to please a woman. Little does he know I know exactly how to please

Maggie.

The wind picks up, making our napkins tumble across our table and fly off in the night air, leaving a chill running down my spine. The feeling that something dreadful is going to happen crawls over me. When the waitress appears with our wine, I shake off the notion.

"Friends of yours?" Maggie asks.

"Yes. We're all part of the Fallen Saints. The one talking to you was Cutter. Shadow is the biggest of them and then J-Bird is our president. They're a great bunch of guys," which they are. We all mess with each other and the best part is we get over it. There's only been a handful of times where we boxed it out in the backyard at the clubhouse.

"Hmm," Maggie narrows her eyes at my wine when I sip on it. "I can't believe you're not drinking beer or a hard liquor," Maggie states.

"What makes you think I don't enjoy wine?" I ask, picking up my glass as I take another sip, letting it sit on my tongue, savoring the taste.

She shrugs, "I just had you pegged for liking beer or something harder," she says honestly.

Most women don't say what is on their mind and I find it refreshing that she does. I admire that about her. She doesn't seem to give a shit about what others think. Strong, a business professional, and a body for fucking makes her a catch.

"I'm full of all kinds of surprises, Pussycat."

A soft vibration occurs on the table and Maggie

picks up her phone to view it. Disappointment crosses her beautiful features.

"Is everything okay?" I curiously ask. I'm ready to take action if she needs me to kick ass.

"Yeah," she puts the phone face down on the table. "I haven't received a call from the client I told you about. The one that I was supposed to go to next. He's either found someone cheaper or..." she trails off, lost in her thoughts.

I reach across the table interlacing our fingers, "I'm positive it had nothing to do with you," I tell her, leaving out the part where I told her new client he needed to find someone else, and that he wasn't to contact her. If he did, then I would see to it his business would take a nose-dive right into bankruptcy. She doesn't need to know that part.

"I'm only supposed to work for you one more week. I need to start making a few calls and get another job lined up," she mentions, as if I plan on letting her leave in a week.

"No need. I can use the help as long as you are willing to stay. Paperwork is not my forte. I would rather be out behind the bar and now that I have a full staff again, I'm able to take time off as much as I like to spend time with you."

The way her face lit up and her eyes shine when I mention spending time with her makes me want to spend every minute making sure that smile doesn't leave her face.

Our plates are set down on our table with the

platters overflowing with shrimp, scallops, the fresh catch of the day, and side dishes of fries, coleslaw, and variety of sides to go along with the meat. Maggie's eyes widen.

"Wow, you weren't kidding. This is huge," she says with excitement in her voice.

We finish the platter, with Maggie eating most of the food. Who knew a woman could eat like that. We headed down the stairs on the patio to take a walk along the beach. I wrap my arm around her, letting my hand rest on her shoulder. She fits perfect by my side. When we get farther away from the busy area, I stop walking and sit down on the sand.

"Take a seat," I pat my lap, encouraging her to sit.

She looks around us, but there's no one in sight.

"Come on Maggie. Don't worry, no one is going to see us."

Lifting her dress, she straddles me, giving me a front and center view of her breasts, making me growl. Her nipples are hard, and I finally get a taste after being teased all evening by them. Slowing, lowering the thin straps of her dress, I gently pull them down when her hands fly up to stop me.

"Someone is going to see us," she mumbles. She's as turned on as I am, if the way she's grinding on my lap is any indication.

"Baby, no one's here and if they were, they would know better than to look at what's mine."

She's still trying to hold my hands, afraid someone is in the dark watching us. I take her mouth in a heated kiss, hoping to relieve the tension in her body. Slowly, I kiss her and with each tongue stroke; she relaxes more. My fingers slide under the small straps of her dress, pulling them down her arms until her large nipples are exposed. Grabbing them with both hands, I give them a squeeze.

"Fuckkk, I'm a titty man and these girls are perfect."

I slide one nipple into my mouth, moaning, sucking, and licking around it while I pinch and roll the other one. When I pop it out of my mouth, I blow on the hard nub, making goosebumps cover her skin.

"Does my Pussycat like that?" I ask, smiling into her eyes.

I give the other nipple the same attention, licking and kissing my way up to her mouth, "Are you wet for me?"

Maggie hums and presses her sweet cunt harder down against my cock.

Sliding one hand to her thigh, I push my way up to her core, "Holy fuck, Pussycat. You don't have any panties on," my dick is so fucking hard. I had no idea she was bare underneath her dress. No wonder she didn't want her legs spread. Thank fuck, this dress is long enough to cover her cunt or I would have had to kill someone if they saw her.

Her hands dig into my shoulders.

"Are you ready to get fucked?" I unzip my jeans. "Lift up a little so I can pull my jeans down enough to free my cock for you to ride on."

Once I have my dick out, I hold it up for her. She inserts the head of my dick into her sweetness, making me moan. Putting my hands on her hips, I urge her to let me in all the way. Her eyes hold mine and she fucking grins at me. Teasing the hell out of my dick, then with all the force she has, she slams down on my length, causing me to almost jump out of my fucking skin because it feels so damn good.

"Holy shit, Pussycat," I hiss.

"Did you like that?" she teases me. "Do you think you have what it takes to tame this Pussy... cat?"

I'm about to come just from that dirty mouth she has on her.

"What a dirty mouth you have Pussycat. I just might have to wash is out with my dick if you don't shut up and ride this big cock."

CHAPTER 21

Maggie

Colt and I walk along the beach back to the restaurant's parking lot. My skin prickles the closer we get to the car. The unwanted nerves of being watched hit me like a cold splash of freezing water to the face.

"Hey," Colt cups my face. "Talk to me… relax," his words are soft but they're not helping. His lips brush mine and it has the same effect as it did when we were on the beach. It brings me out of my head and into the moment enjoying his big plump lips as they take my bottom lip into his mouth, igniting all my girl parts.

This man has become more than something to look at like the gorgeous posters I used to put on my wall as a teenager. He's deeper and more caring than I could have ever given him credit for. I've always been more interested in men older than me, thinking they could give me the stability and security I've always desired in a man, but Colt has definitely proven that age is just a number. He's everything wrapped up in a package that would make any woman swoon at his feet.

"HEY!" someone yells, causing me to jump into Colt's arms.

A deep belly laugh follows. Colt and I both turn to see two of his friends laughing, falling over one another. They must be drunk with how they are carrying on. The one he called Shadow stands to the side, watching something on his cell phone.

"I'm..." Cutter laughs, trying to get his words out. He continues, "Oh shit, you..." he bends over holding his stomach, "should have seen you."

The smell of alcohol fans in my face, making me want to give them a can of breath mints. After a few moments of getting their giggles out of their system, Cutter and J-Bird finally get their composure straight and are able to talk more clearly.

"Oh shit, that was funny! Why don't you bring your woman back to the clubhouse? There's a party going on and you can introduce her to the others," Cutter says with a grin that reeks of sin.

When Colt doesn't reply, my heart sinks. What if he's just using me for sex? I hate to think of it, but it's happened to me before, what makes me think this man could be any different?

He wraps his large arms around me, whispering in my ear, "Stop. Don't over think shit. I was wanting to have you all to myself but if you don't mind and only if you want to go, we will," I swear it's like he knows me better than anyone ever has.

Allowing myself to relax and melt into his arms, "Yeah, that would be nice," unsure if it will be anything, but it might be nice to meet a bunch of bikers and see woman that I have no doubt I will be scratching their eyes out if they look longer than necessary at Colt. Jealousy is ugly and I can be the definition of it if provoked. I have no problem taking down an exhaust pipe hopping skank if I need to.

Everyone agrees to meet back up at the clubhouse as we leave the parking lot. Colt and I are riding in his truck. Reaching across the console, he grabs my hand and places it on his thigh.

"I want you touching me," he says when he places my hand on the upper thigh.

My hand is close enough to his cock that all I would need to do is stretch out my pinky to brush against it.

My god, this man!

"How long before we get there?" I ask, curious if it's close.

He doesn't answer as a call comes through on the speakers and lights up Dad on the radio screen.

"Dad," Colt answers.

"Colt, hope I'm not interrupting anything," Connor says, and I can tell he's smiling.

Colt looks over to me, lifting my hand to kiss my fingers, "Nope, just finished," Colt's eyes light up and I swat his shoulder.

Connor chuckles, "We forgot to mention we're going to close up the pool and put the boats away after Labor Day weekend and wanted you and Maggie to come up."

Colt looks at me, raising his eyebrows. I know he's asking if I will be okay seeing Charles. My palms sweat at the thought of having to be in the same room with him. Now I'm going to have to think about sitting at the same table as Charles and Connie. Great fun that'll be. If I want to be with Colt, I have to get used to being around Charles and Connie. So, there's nothing like ripping off the band-aid. So I give Colt a nod, letting him know I can handle it.

"We'll be there but I have a request."

"What is it?"

"Maggie and I are staying in the same room. No separate rooms," Colt says firmly.

"Well," Connor says with a laugh. "I wouldn't expect any less of you than to not want to let a woman like that out of your sight. Then, it's set. Come early if you can. We'll be arriving on Wednesday before the weekend."

By the end of their conversation, we are at an older home that has at least fifty bikes parked in front of it along with muscle cars. There are women standing along the steps to enter the house with very little fabric covering their privates.

"They'll ride anything," Colt comments.

He must have noticed how my eyes haven't left the women standing at the end of the steps. I close my mouth to keep from making a comment. I'm not sure if I'm jealous at some of the women being prettier than I imagined, or if it's the thought of Colt sleeping with someone that's more available to him than I am.

I close my eyes and will these self doubts to be push away to the far back of my mind.

I am good enough. Any man should be honored to be with me. I deserve—.

"Maggie… Maggie," Colt's voice brings me out of my chant.

I open my eyes turning my head to him when a large lifted truck pulls up to Colt's side and parks.

"We won't stay long. I'll introduce you to a few guys and then we'll head to my room," he pulls me in to place a soft kiss on my lips. "Then I'll—.

Bang, Bang. Cutter hits the window and without looking, Colt shoots him a bird. It doesn't stop him from hitting the window again.

"Get your ass out and come on," Cutter slurs his words.

"Cut-ter," a voice purrs out of Colt's window.

It's the brunette that was standing with a few other women at the end of the steps. She flutters her eyelashes and I think she's about to take flight with how long they are.

Less is more.

"Ser… Serena," Cutter finally says her name correctly in his drunken state.

I notice when Cutter says her name, Colt sinks his head into his shoulders, and it makes me wonder if he's been with her.

He rolls up his window all the way, blocking out what they are talking about, "You ready to head in?"

Reaching for the door handle, he stops me, "Hold still. I'll get it."

When he gets out of the truck the brunette tries to stop him, but he keeps walking, ignoring her. I definitely think something is there.

We head inside with Cutter and J-Bird behind us. I have no idea where Shadow went. He seems like a nice enough guy, but scary enough to want to keep distance from him.

"Do you want a beer?" Colt yells over the music when we make it inside of the house.

"Yeah."

He starts to walk off from me, but I tag along. There's no way I want to be left here alone. We're rounding the corner to the kitchen when a small body slams into Colt.

"Nat!" Colt sounds excited to see his beach neighbor. The same girl that was riding Charles' dick, my ex-boyfriend, the last time I saw her.

"Oh my god, Colt!" She leaps into his arms like they are long lost pen pals. "Do you know some of the Fallen Saints?" she asks.

Why do I have a feeling she planned this? There's no way that little cunt didn't know he was in the club. Their families have been neighbors for years.

"You could say that. Aren't you supposed to be in school?"

Colt's large frame blocks Nat from seeing me standing behind him. Is he just as Nat crazy as Charles was? I shake my head. No, there's no one as crazy as Charles was for her.

"I transferred to CU and I'm in my last semester. I'll be a graduate soon!" her high pitched voice just about bursts my ear drums.

"Who are you here with?"

"Johnny Tolbert," her small fingers point past Colt to a guy standing talking to a couple.

It's the same guy that I thought busted my side-view mirror.

Oh good lord, I hope he doesn't see me.

I look closer at the couple he's talking to. Her skirt is covering the man's lap, leaving nothing to the imagination when she slowly rises and slides back down.

Yep, they're having open sex and acting completely normal about it.

My lip has a mind of its own and curls in horror. Why would she be so willing to ride his dick in a room full of people?

"Don't look so turned off. I'll have you riding mine in a few minutes, but it'll be in the privacy of my room," Colt's words send a wave of heat straight to my core.

Damn him and his sinful words.

"You remember Nat?" A smile that looks more forced tugs on the corners of Nat's face.

Do I remember the girl who I last saw riding my ex-

boyfriend's cock? Yes, yes, I do.

"Yes," I put on a fake as hell smile grinning right back at her.

I'm thankful when Cutter places his arm on my shoulder, "You want a drink?"

Hell yes!

"Love one," I say it with hopes that I can get out of this awkward moment.

The blame is not on Nat, but she should apologize for not being able to control herself enough not to go to bed with a guy that has a girlfriend.

"I'm borrowing your girlfriend," Cutter pulls me to a bar where a young guy is working.

Cutter orders us some drinks but I'm to focused on the heat on the back of my neck burning me. Glancing over my shoulder at Colt, his sharp laser eyes are shooting me a deadly stare. Crap! I didn't think he would mind if I walked a few feet away just to grab a drink. He looks to Cutter, and he narrows his eyes, making his eyes appear darker. I can tell Nat is getting flustered trying to get his attention. She moves to stand in front of him, but his height gives him the advantage to look over the top of her head.

He says something to her then steps aside and walks in long strides over to me. Pulling a bar stool out he sits down to my side. His large hands wrap around my waist, jerking me back to sit on his lap.

"Don't ever walk away from me with another man," his lips sweep over the shell of my ear. "Doesn't matter who they are," he says as he licks my ear, making shivers run down my back.

I grind my ass on his lap, "Didn't think you would notice with old Nat being here," I bite out.

He couldn't expect me to stand there and make nice with her, could he? Why would he think I would want to stand there and talk sweet with her. Nat and I are nothing alike. Unlike her, I have my self-respect. I don't sleep with anyone's boyfriend or husband. Well, at least not that I know of. If they lie, then it's technically not my fault. She knew I was with Charles and still slept with him.

Colts' hands dig into my hips, "If you keep doing that, I'm going to unload right here in my pants." My mind thinks about how that couple that was openly having sex. I wonder if Colt has had public sex before?

A sharp pain pierces my hands. I didn't realize my hands were balled into fists. Opening my hands, there's a faint color of red. Just thinking of Colt with another woman brings out my jealous side. I was never this jealous over Charles or any man I'd dated before Colt.

"Here you go," Cutter sets a shot down in front of me.

Before I can grab it, Colt takes it, tossing it back.

"Where's Serena?" Colt breath fans my skin.

"Don't know," Cutter shrugs his shoulders, then grabs another one of the five shots lined up in front of him, slamming it back and placing the empty glass down. He continues with the next shot in line.

"Hmm," is all Colt comments.

Colt pushes my hair to one side of my neck while his lips nip, lick, and suck on the bare skin. Any other time I would close my eyes completely and enjoy the way his lips feel on my skin, but there's a nagging in the back of my head that won't allow me to.

My eyes scan the room out of habit. I've always made assumptions about bikers. It's wrong of me to judge others just because of a few bad apples. I can see that now. Dating Colt has cleared that up. A biker can be responsible, caring, and a fucking fantastic lover. There's just… a small voice in the back of my brain that keeps nagging at me, telling me there are so many bodies in this place that you never will know what might happen. A fight, a shootout, my mind goes wild with too many different temperaments being crammed in this small room. I feel… unsafe for some reason. It's the same feeling I get walking by myself in dark parking lots or on a dark street. The same feeling that someone may jump out of the blue and cause me harm. When my eyes land on a set of cold hard eyes watching me and Colt too closely, I knew my instincts were right.

"Colt," A deep voice booms a few feet from us, making me jump out of the imprisonment the woman had on me.

Johnny, the guy Nat came here with, the same handsome face that I thought had hit my car with his bike was walking over to us with a sexy as hell smile on his face. Nat is still standing up against the wall where he left her. I wonder how long they have been dating?

"How's it going man?" Colt calls back.

I tuck my head down, praying to God above he doesn't recognize me. He's standing beside us, blocking the small pathway which is the only space to escape. The other option would to be crawl over the bar and I'm by far not above doing it.

Johnny does some kind of hand shake with Colt, causing Colt's warmth to leave my backside. In the short time we've been together, I've grown to love the way his body fits around mine. He never wastes any opportunity to touch me. Once they're finished with their bro hand shake and patting each other on the back, Colt wraps himself back around me, making me feel secure.

Johnny's forest green eyes collide with mine and I shrink a little. I didn't mean to make contact but couldn't help but stare at how dark his eyes are.

"So..." he says staring at me with that fuck me smile on his face. "Have you yelled at anymore drivers?"

Shit, I knew he would remember. It's not every day you run into a crazy lady on the interstate yelling you messed up her car.

"Not lately," Colt's body tenses behind me. I turn to him to say, "I kind of blamed your friend for breaking my wing mirror, but I didn't realize it folds." I tell Colt honestly.

Johnny laughs, breaking the weirdness between us.

"No big deal. I get accused of shit all the time. It wouldn't be the first time someone has chased me down. It won't be the last I'm sure," he states like the trouble maker I thought he would be when I first saw him.

"I'd like to talk to you in private," he says to Colt.

Pretending I didn't hear I ask him, "How long have you been dating Nat?" I can't help but want to know if it's serious.

"Who?" Johnny asks with confusion on his face.

Seriously, does she go by a different name? Or does he really not know her name?

"The girl that's been by your side all night," I cock an eyebrow.

He looks over to Nat shrugging his shoulders, "Oh yeah, met her today. I was riding through town and she flagged me down wanting a ride on my bike... among other things," he snickers.

Asshole.

"I'll be back in a few minutes," Colt breathes into my ear, standing up.

All the women in the room turn when Colt and Johnny pass by to walk down a long hallway. The same woman who was hanging on Cutter earlier in the night, Serena, comes around the corner at the end of the hallway, stopping in front of the guys. She slides her hand up Colt's chest. I watch to see how he'll react, hoping he does the right thing because if he doesn't, I'm out. I can't and will not be a fool again. Not for all the dick in the world.

When Colt grabs her hand before she reaches his pecs and shoves it away, I smile.

Good boy.

Her lips press in a tight grimace before she shoves him to the side with her shoulder.

I guess some people don't handle rejection too well.

Cutter stands in front of me, laughing and talking to a woman that has eased up to his side. Good for him, maybe it's just what he needs.

It's not long before Colt comes back, lacing our hands together and tugging me to the hallway where he disappeared earlier. No words are said until we come to a door. He unlocks it and drags me in with him.

There is a small bar in the corner and a door adjacent to the room that's open. I can see it's a bathroom. The black comforter covering the king size bed isn't anything fancy, but it suits Colt. The whole vibe reminds me of my college dorm days except this room is much larger.

"Get naked and lay down," Colts says in a raspy voice.

I unzip the back of my dress, letting it fall to the floor. He already knows I wasn't wearing any under clothes, so he's not surprised to see me naked because of the sex on the beach earlier tonight.

I climb on the bed and lay flat on my back, stretching my arms above my head.

"Spread your legs I'm about to eat my weight in pussy."

CHAPTER 22

Colt

Heavy thundering footsteps jar me awake as they come crashing down the hallway. Maggie's sleeping in front of me, with my nose buried into her hair. Her soft snores fill the room, but they're quickly drowned out when loud banging occurs on my bedroom door, causing Maggie's eyes to open wide. She shoots up into a sitting position, letting the sheet drop off her.

"It's okay baby, lay still and keep the cover over you," slipping out of the bed I grab my briefs from the floor. Turning around, I glance at my clock beside the bed and see it's three in the morning. Maggie lays back down pulling the sheet up to her chin and rolls over facing away from the door. Another round of banging happens, and I curse out loud. Whoever this is it better be good.

"What the fuck—" I open the door to see Jay, Shadow, and Cutter crowding around the door. I shouldn't be worried, I'm used to shit going down this early in the morning, but their faces are contorted with anger and sympathy. "Something wrong?" I ask, stepping out into the hallway, closing the door behind me. I don't want any of these fuckers to see Maggie naked or I'll lose my shit.

"Get your clothes on. Someone broke into the bar and smashed the place up," Jay tells me, making me almost lose my footing.

"My bar?" I point my finger to my chest, stricken with disbelief.

"It had to have happened not to long after I closed up. I forget my phone when I got back to the clubhouse. When I went back, the windows were busted. I went inside and saw a bat laying on the bar," he raises it up from his side. I hadn't even seen it until now.

My heart hurts like a semi-truck crashed through it, shattering it to pieces. Cutter is the closest to me, he lays his large palm over my shoulder giving it a squeeze.

"I promise you brother, we're going to find out who did this. Shadow said we can watch the footage from the security system he put in. Whoever this fucker is, he doesn't know who he's messing with."

Anger fuels my body, "I swear I'll going to kill whoever did this," my fist balls up and I punch the wall with my good arm. The pain isn't enough to numb the anger, hurt, and betrayal I feel. Anger because I recognize that ball bat. It's signed by one of the greatest baseball players of all time. My dad took us to see Cory Lee's last game of his career. Charles being the crybaby he was, had to have the bat when it was mine to begin with. I'm hurt that he would betray his own family. We're not blood but we're supposed to be family, since his mom married my dad.

"We'll meet you out front," Jay tilts his head down the hallway. All three large men walk away, leaving me trying to calm my nerves before I go back to Maggie.

My bar was my livelihood, my sanctuary, and the one place I felt at peace. All the chaos from the rowdy customers, the employees who have come and gone were like a welcoming mat that I looked forward to everyday. I live for it. Now someone has invaded my holy place and I plan on making them pay with more than just words.

When I walk into the room, Maggie's standing in the open bathroom already dressed.

"Where are you going?" my words are rough. They're harsh and cold, but it wasn't my intent to come out as an ass to her. "I don't want you to leave," I say with sincerity. It's the truth, I want her to stay in my bed until I get back, but I can't tell she's not going to stay put.

She walks over to me, "I heard you talking. I'm sorry," her empathy makes me want to crumble to the floor.

I run a hand through my hair. This is too much,

first with Maggie almost getting run down, Dad getting sick and now my bar being trashed. There has to be something that is linking them all together. Charles. It's Charles. The problem is no one knows where the little fucker is.

Maggie looks at me with those big eyes filled with sympathy. I know what she's thinking before she says anything.

"No. This is not your fault. Someone is playing with fire and they're about to get incinerated. The guys are waiting for me outside. Crawl back into my bed and wait for me. I just need to go and see the damage. We're going to look at the video footage, and I'll have to fill out a police report for the insurance," I pause to see if she's going to crawl back into the bed. When she doesn't say anything, I tell her, "I don't want you going home right now. Stay here. J-Bird will be here and some other guys that will protect you. Somebody would have to be stupid to try any shit here."

She reaches up on her tip toes, bringing her soft lips to mine. My hand reaches around her neck and into her hair line, bringing her closer to deepen the kiss. We stand beside the bed, our tongues slowly exploring each other. Her body melts into mine and I want nothing more than to throw her back onto the bed and kiss every inch of her body.

Breaking out kiss, I reluctantly pull away, "I have to go. Tell me you'll stay."

She nods her head, "Go take care of your bar. I'll

be here when you get back."

After I get dress and kiss Maggie goodbye, I head outside to where the guys are waiting. I'm in a shit mood compared to earlier tonight. Bitterness lines my stomach like acid. My bar. My fucking bar has been trashed like it's nothing, and today of all days someone smashes it. The worst day of the year for me. Today is the anniversary of my mother's death. Thirteen years has gone and each day that goes by, her memory fades out more. Bits and pieces of her are slowly dwindling from my mind.

I normally go to the cemetery alone on this day, but with what happened this morning I may be making my annual trip later than expected. My dad doesn't go. I've never seen flowers other than the ones I leave on her grave. A part of him died along with her that frightful day. He's never truly recovered from her death.

"Maggie staying?" Jay asks, scaring the shit out of me. I was expecting everyone to be outside, not lurking in the dark corner of the living room.

"Shit! You startled me. I thought everyone was outside."

"Cutter and Shadow went to the bar. We weren't sure how long you would be. I told them to go on. I'd wait," there's a dullness to his voice that's full of regret and remorse.

"You know this isn't your fault," I give his shoulder a squeeze.

Shaking his head he looks up to me his expression

silently pleading me to forgive him, but there's nothing to forgive. He's not the one to blame.

"I feel like it is."

"It's not. Come on, let's go find out who the real dead man walking is."

The bar is lit up like Christmas when we arrive, blue lights are flashing a half a mile away. The sight of blue lights is never a good sign on any given day, but today is different. Today I'm thankful they're here. I need there report to help me out with my insurance claim. I've sunk all my money into the bar, leaving very little in savings. What I have left I've got to pay Shadow for his work on the apartment I'm having built upstairs.

My boots crunch on the broken glass under my feet. The sight of broken bottles and tumblers along with tables that have been turned over has me about to hurl, but with all the turmoil what has me the most repulsed is the fact this asshole took a shit on top of the bar.

I pick up the leg of a bar stool and throw it across the room, hitting one of the pool tables sitting along the wall. "Fuck!" kicking the wall, I curse out again.

The officers just let me have this moment because I need it. I need Charles in front of me so I can beat the living fuck out of him. The wild animal in me wants to go rogue, to destroy everything in sight. Feeding the rage with destruction is the only way I'm going to be tamed again. I kick the table top that's tipped over on the floor.

"Mother fucker! I'm going to kick your ass when I find you," I yell out as I continue my assault on my broken furniture.

Several minutes of screaming to release the hurt that bubble up from within, I collapse on the only bar stool that still is in good shape.

"Feel better?" the dark headed officer asks.

Shooting him a don't fuck with me glare, he clears his throat and pulls out a small note book and pen. "I just need to ask a few questions," he comments looking down. He doesn't look me in the eye. Good. That uniform that rests on his back couldn't save him if I was to jump up and rip him apart because of his smart mouth.

"Any idea who could have done this?"

I click my tongue, "No idea," my mouth closes. I'm not trying to protect Charles. It's my dad that I'm trying to save. Even if they put Charles in jail, it'll be my dad who will have to bail him out. He's already wasted enough of my dad's money.

"Anyone you know of who might have a vendetta against you?"

Jay speaks up, "He just fired an employee named Nina Flagstone," Jay's eyes narrow at me, silently telling me to say something.

I highly doubt Nina could have gotten Charles' bat, but if I want to save my dad the headache, I'll go with it. "She wasn't happy with her termination. It was a few nights back, but she came in and brought her boyfriend trying to start crap."

The officer takes notes, looking around, pointing his pen up in the corner of the bar, "You've got a security camera," it's more of a statement than a question.

"Yeah, we were going to look at it," getting off the bar stool, I motion for him to come to the office.

I stop at the door that leads into my small office. It's trashed. The filing cabinet I have is open, all the papers are torn and dispersed over the floor. The old leather couch that wasn't worth anything is ripped up. Panic laces my nerve endings. My apartment. I run up the stairs two at a time, swinging the door open. It's in bad shape but nothing like downstairs. There are holes punched in the new sheet rock, and I can see where they tried to rip out wires but thought otherwise. I guess they were too afraid of getting an electric shock. Which only leads me to believe this was more than a one-person job. I'm guessing whoever did this was waiting on Jay to leave, given the amount of damage that was done in a short time period.

Shadow stands behind me, "I can have this fixed up in no time," his deep voice rumbles. "Let's have a look at that footage."

He's distracting me from the disappointment of everything crashing down on me. My chest rises and falls when I blow out air that I've held since I ran up the stairs.

"Yeah, let's go," closing the door on my shock and disbelief of my dreams being wrecked, I head downstairs with a new determination. Fink Charles and fuck his up!

Soon everyone is gathered around a table, watching the surveillance video on my laptop. I give myself a mental pat on the back for always locking it up in the wall safe. If I hadn't there's no way it would have survived and since it has all my personal and business information on it, that would have sucked ass if it had been stolen or bashed.

The video starts playing, showing nothing at first. Then a dark figure comes onto the screen. They're dressed in all black with their face covered. Squinting my eyes, I move closer to the screen. I can't tell if the figure is a male or female.

"Can anyone see if that figure has tits?" Cutter blurs out.

"If it does it's a sad pair," Shadow gives his two cents.

I'm not disagreeing with them, but I sure as hell don't care if they have tits or not. All my attention is drawn to their face. I can't make out shit. The cameras are supposed to have infrared technology but it's not helping with details. I can't make out if it's a man or woman. The only thing that I can tell certain is whoever it is has a trim figure.

The unidentified person looks up at the camera at an angle then moves closer, keeping their head down. I'm gripping the edge of the table when they get close to the camera. If they will just get close enough, maybe I can see their eye color or make out the color of their hair. But when they move suddenly out of the camera's view right before they get close enough for me to make out details, I release the edge of the table.

Fuck!

The top of a toboggan pops up in sight right before the camera goes out. *They've cut the line.* I push away from the table screaming, "Fucking hell."

After reviewing all the other camera's video, we still have nothing. The unidentified person knew their way around the bar. Which means they're more than likely a repeating customer. There's no way they could have known where all the cameras were just by visiting once or twice.

I've never known Charles to come to the bar. He wouldn't know his way out of a paper sack much less around my bar. The only person that would know their way around would be Nina. I thought the night she brought her boy toy here we scared her enough to warn her off, but it doesn't appear that way. Maybe it's time to pay her a visit and do more than talk.

CHAPTER 23

Maggie

My eyes are closed, and my body is still but sleep still doesn't come. I've been laying here for hours, and my mind is occupied with thoughts of Colt. I could feel the hurt and anger he was feeling radiating from his body to mine. I wanted to go with him, to give him the emotional support he needed, but I knew he would be worried about me the entire time we were there. He's too agitated to handle anything rational. The way he was snapping at me when he walked back in the room, agreeing to stay behind was the best decision I could make to keep him from coming apart. At least I keep telling myself that.

My phone pings from across the room, and I scramble up out of bed, hoping it's a message from Colt. I need it to from him. I'm going out of my mind with worry. The sun is starting to rise, and I haven't heard a word from him.

I swipe the screen to open a message from a number that appears to be blocked. My breath hitches when photos appear on the screen. It's photos of Colt's bar. Metal signs that once decorated the walls now dress the floor. The black and white vintage sign of the bar's name tells me it's definitely Colt's bar. All the beautiful tumblers that lined the mirror wall all have been destroyed along with the mirror.

I zoom in closer on a picture that is a section of the bar. Nothing really looks different, except when I zoom in, I'm disgusted by the shot. My face curls up in horror that someone would sink so low as to have a bowel movement on the beauty butcher block countertop. My muscles tighten up from irritation from the lack of respect for someone's property. If I'm feeling this way, I can't imagine how Colt is feeling.

My hand curls around the phone and I throw it onto the bed. Sickened by the pictures, I start to pace the floor. I need to see Colt. I need to see if he's okay. By the fifth time of pacing, the door clicks and it opens to see an unrecognizable Colt. His clothes are a mess, they're dirty and sweaty from hours of work. His face has beads of sweat dripping from his hair line and the expression on his face is a mixture of anger and defeat.

Crossing the room to greet him, I approach with caution. The events of this morning hold a great magnitude on his mood. We stand face to face, no words, just staring into each other's eyes. Slowly I take the hem of his t-shirt and lift it over his head. He needs a shower and I plan on helping to bathe him, and release the tension that's in his muscles in a soaking hot tub.

"Let me help you," he nods giving his approval but there's vulnerability in his eyes.

I pull him to the bathroom, placing the toilet lid down and asking him to sit. Once I get the bath started, I pull his shoes and socks off one by one.

"Stand up for me," I ask on bended knee in front of him.

He stands, his eyes never leaving mine. As I unbutton and unzip his pants, I wonder if I've ever felt this way for someone. Even when Charles was at his lowest point, I didn't feel the need or even the want to take the time to make sure his emotions were my number one priority.

"Step out of your jeans and slide into the tub," my voice is strained.

His large cock bobs in my face. He's hard. I want to wrap my lips around his length and swallow him down my throat, but right now is not the time, he's broken.

When he finally settles against the back of the tub, he looks back at me, waiting to see what I do next. It takes everything in me not to want to join him.

"Close your eyes and relax, let the heat of the water release the tension in your body."

I start to walk away but he stops me, "Join me. The only thing I need right now is you," his words send ripples of tingles down my spine and to my core.

Without hesitation, I undress with his full attention on me and step over the large tub, settling in front of him. His arms wrap around me, pulling me against him. He dips his face into my neck, kissing my shoulder.

"Thank you," he whispers into my ear.

"You don't have to thank me," my words are filled with sincerity. I would and will take care of this man for as long as he'll let me.

"No one hasn't done anything for me like this since my mother," his voice cracks.

"What about Connie? Did she not..." my words die off. The tears in my eyes build up when I feel his head shake. Of course, Connie is too much invested on her and Charles status to care about her husband's son. The man she pledged her loyalty to on the day she married him.

Colt sucks in a large breath of air then blows it across my skin, leaving goosebumps in the wake, "Today of all days," his head leaves my neck and I hear it thump against the tub.

My brows pinch together at his comment, "What is today?"

The muscles under his beautiful golden skin flex, "My mother's anniversary. Her death anniversary."

I close my eyes and curse under my breath. Angling my body, I bring my lips to his, whispering as they brush together, "I'm so sorry. I wish I could take your pain away," placing a small kiss on his lips, I pull back to see the heat in his eyes.

"Maggie," his chest rises. "I have so many emotions running rapid through my body right now. I don't want to use you for just a fuck, and that's what this would be right now," his words are rough.

My feelings are the same as they were when he walked back into this room. Taking care of him will always be my first primary focus. Colt's anger would be put to good use between my legs, that much I'm sure of.

"Use my body then. I can handle it… I want it."

There's a rumble in his chest before he stands up, carrying me with him to the bed room. We're both dripping water across the floor before he throws me on the bed. He grabs my ankles, yanking me down to the edge of the bed. His hard angry cock stands ready to unleash on me. I would give him my soul if it meant that I could help him.

He raises my legs up to be line up with my body, then pushes himself into me. "Oh Pussycat," his eyes close when he's fully inside of me. Opening his eyes, there's emotions of anger, betrayal, sadness, and fear lingering in his eyes. They move from his heart to mine, allowing me to feel his pain from losing his mother all those years ago. Then with a switch of a blink he hides them, breaking the link where they ran between us.

He pushes me up the bed just enough to climb onto the edge, bending down to bring my legs with him, kissing me with intense need to be close, to tangle our bodies into one. Our tongues dance with one another and the heat between my legs come to a boil. When he breaks away his face looks like he's hurt. As he starts back to fucking me, he pounds into me so hard I have to hold onto the sheets.

"Fuck, fuck, fuck!" he says under his breath. "I'm not going to be able to wait for you," his eyes search for understanding. This isn't about me. Not right now. This is about me giving him what he needs to come back from the lost depths of his thoughts. I nod my head, unable to speak as I give him permission to use me as he needs to.

As if he was waiting for my permission, he pushes himself as far as possible into me, groaning from his release, filling me up with the release of all his unwanted energy.

Collapsing on me, he places kisses up and down my neck, "I need a moment," he remarks. Colt's body starts to crush me, and I think he's gone to sleep. Mustering up the strength, I try to push him off me. "My dick isn't ready to leave home yet," he says, surprising me with the amusement in his voice.

Whatever is happening between us is greater than I ever expected. Him opening up to me about his mother was more of a giant leap between us that I've never had from anyone in my past. It's a sign of his comfortable state with me. A sign of the trust he's given to me.

"Home?" I laugh. I love this side of him. Playful, charming, and dirty as hell when he talks. "You're kind of crushing me," I poke him in the side. His face has a smile on it that lights up my insides.

He rolls off to lay beside me, interlacing our fingers when he lays flat on his back, "Come with me today to the cemetery?" he asks, looking up at the ceiling.

My heart gets stuck in my throat, ready to jump out. This is it. This between us is what love could be, sharing our lows and highs. Being there for each other when everything around us is crumbling. When you feel like it's hard to breathe, and all you want to do is to crawl under the covers while you let the day go by. Never seeing sunshine. Never looking toward anything positive.

"Yes," I'm not sure if it really was a question, but I answer it like it was. The excitement crashes into me as I crawl ontop of him.

"I can never get enough of your big fat dick," I smile, knowing it's true and hoping to lighten the mood. It works, when his strong jaw line spreads into a smoking panty melting smile.

CHAPTER 24

Colt

I watch the pink and gold casket lower into the dark damp grave. A tear falls from my cheek, chasing it. Prayers and well wishes of a better tomorrow have been said over my mom's body. I don't feel the promises of greater things to come, only the loneliness to fill the minutes and hours of each passing day.

People come by and hug us; I keep my head down, barely able to register the words they say. An hour passes by when I look up to my dad. He's as stiff as a statue, unmoving, eyes set straight and void. I wonder if his spirit was buried along with mom. I know mine is. My spirit left the day the doctor told us that she died.

My feet have been carrying me around today, but my mind has been in a fog. I'm not even sure how I made it to stand over my mother's casket.

Extending my hand, I let go of the white rose letting it fall till it lands on the emboss flowers carved on top of the casket. I fight back the cry that wants to rip out of me. Why my mom?

Why her?

Every year I visit mother's grave, I get the same vision, me standing over her grave wishing she wasn't laying under six feet of dirt. How can you bury someone when you can't say goodbye? I was too young to say goodbye. I shouldn't have had to say those words. The word is like glass that slices at my insides. If I have to say it to another loved one, I know it'll finish what it started years ago.

Maggie squeezes my hand, "Colt," her soft voice calls. "It's starting to rain hard," she's right. The rain is coming down in heavy sheets of tears, even God is crying for my loss.

I drop the white rose I brought on top of the marble tombstone I helped pick out for mom. Its beautiful black marble has a dull effect, mimicking how I feel. She loved the sleekness of the marble counter tops that were in our old house. The same house that Connie had to sell.

Connie claimed the house was too small for our growing family. The problem was our family never grew once her and Charles moved in. Even if we had stayed in our house, the one my mother's memory lives in, it was more than large enough with its five bedrooms and four baths. Connie used every excuse to kill any longing my dad had for my mother's memory to stay alive. Ensuring she was the only one he put his attention on, along with his money.

One last deep breath and I walk away from mother's grave. I don't run even as the rain beats down on me. I'll never run from the emptiness that has a permanent spot in my heart but with Maggie in my future, maybe it can help not ache like a festering sore. Her presence has dulled the pain I normally have in my chest when I visit mom's grave.

Before I open Maggie's car door, I pull her into my chest slide my hands between her soaked blouse and her cold skin. My lips take hers in a kiss that tells her I want her. I want everything she'll give me because I don't think I can breathe without her.

When I pull back to look into those eyes, the same ones I want to wake up to every morning, I noticed the redness outlining them.

"Hey," my voice is barely a whisper escaping my lips. I swipe under her glasses covered eyes. "No tears. Okay?"

"I'm just..." she shakes her head. "I've never seen you so lost, so vulnerable. I want nothing more than to wrap you up in a bubble and look after you."

A huge smile erupts on my face. No one besides my mother has ever wanted to take care of me like that. My dad has taken care of me all my life, but a woman's love is different. I can picture Maggie as a mother. She would be as protective as a mother hen would be. Demanding the school bully to back off or else.

I huff out a laugh, "Hop in the truck before you get pneumonia."

Her eyebrows are draw together and her lips part, but she doesn't say anything. She steps onto the aluminum step, climbing into the truck. I place my hand on her firm ass, making sure she doesn't slip. She's all smiles, swatting at my hand.

"Colt, I didn't need assistance on my ass," her tone is playful.

I shrug my shoulders, "I can't help my hand likes the firmness of your ass."

Shutting the door, I round the front of the truck to the driver's side. I've got plans to turn this day into pure bliss, and being inside of Maggie is my next stop.

***

"You got a backpack?"

"Yes."

"Good. We're taking my bike, so don't pack a lot," I hold my phone between my ear and chin, talking to Maggie. "You won't need it. I plan to have you naked and wet all weekend," I adjust my cock when I think about her in that leather bikini she has. "Bring that tiny black bikini, I can't wait to peel it off with my teeth."

I've already told my dad that I won't accept a room without Maggie in my bed. To confirm everything was set, I called dad. He mentioned that the pool house would be ours for the week. Maggie's name wasn't mentioned but when I heard something shatter in the background, it didn't take a genius to figure out Connie was listening. She still has no idea it's Maggie I'm going to be shacking up with in her newly renovated pool house. She's going to have a real shit fit. I can already see how her face will be set in shock. It's going to be priceless just to watch her clamp that over bearing tongue and I fucking can't wait.

"My nerves are on high alert," Maggie's voice is shaky. "Are you sure it's okay for me to come? We can wait until you tell both of them about us."

Fuck no!

"I want you there, Mags," I say, stuffing my clothes into my backpack with a little more force. "You don't need to worry. The only person who means shit to me is my dad, and he's cool with us. Trust me," I reassure, pleading with her to overcome her worries on what Connie and Charles will have to say about anything.

She lets out a gust of air.

I know it's weighing on her about Charles being there, but I plan on making it as easy for her as possible. I just need her to meet me halfway in not giving a shit what people say or think and that especially goes for Charles and Connie. This thing between us is real. I feel it, physical and emotional. I need her to trust me that I'll always have her and take care of her.

"Okay."

"Good," I zip my bag and grab the extra helmet I bought for her. Letting her wear the helmet that other women have worn didn't feel right. "I'm headed that way now. Be ready in ten."

When I hang up, I sling my bag over my shoulder, grabbing both helmets making my way out the door.

Thankfully I've got use of both my arms without pain shooting though my shoulder. This week the doctor gave me the go to remove the sling after confirming my collar bone was well enough on its way to healing.

"You out?" Cutter yells from the kitchen doorway.

"Yeah, going to my dads for the weekend."

He gives me a shit eating grin, "Don't eat too much pussy this weekend."

Fucker!

I flip him off before closing the door behind me. His laugh carries to the porch.

The ride is short to Maggie's apartment. I see the front entry way where's she waiting. Dressed in a pair of dark leggings hugging her curves, I groan, she looks like a walking distraction. In my case a riding one. This ride is going to be hard not to stop and fuck her before we get there. Lucky for me, I've got another plan.

Turning the key to switch off my bike, I take off my helmet. "Have you ever driven a bike?"

"Nooo," she says with a slow shake of her head.

I grin, "Today is your lucky day. I'm going to give you a lesson," I lean in. "In more ways than one."

Her cheeks turn pink, letting me know this was the best idea I've ever had.

"Here," I take her backpack and strap it on the back of my Harley. "Climb on," she starts to sit on the back, "No babe, you sit here," I pat the seat in front of me.

"You can't be serious?"

"Dead serious. I'm going to help you. Trust me," I pat the seat again, encouraging her to take the lead.

"Colt," she gives me her 'I'm not doing this' face.

"Maggie," I minace her name. "Get on. You have nothing to worry about. I've got you," she gives in and throws her leg over.

Her plush ass rubs my dick, making it hard. I close my eyes, enjoying the way she's wiggling to get comfortable. If she keeps this up, I won't need to pull over to fuck her. I may be unloading in my pants.

Once we go over all the safety precautions, I lean in and let her know I'm going to help her until we get out of the city. She's a little apprehensive about taking the lead when we get out to an open road, but I know she'll be fine.

I wrap my large frame around her, placing my hands on top of hers on the handle bars, "Just watch me babe," I say into the built in Bluetooth.

The backroads will be a better choice for Maggie to take over, so I decide to jump off the interstate. When we get farther out, I tell Maggie to take over. She's doing great! I can't kiss her neck like I'm dying to, but I let my hands roam over her body.

"Whatever you do, keep driving," I tell her, taking her breasts into my hands. "I fucking love these tits Pussycat."

She hums, almost sounding like a cat purring into my ears. My dick about to jump up and bore a hole in those damn yoga pants. Fucking her up the ass is high on my list. Especially when she's got it plastered up against my cock like she does.

Her body is a little tense as I take my time rolling her nipples between my fingers.

"Relax," I whisper, reminding her again.

I slide my other hand down until I creep under the edge of her yoga pants, "I can't wait to get a taste of this beautiful cunt. I need to sample the goods right now. All you need to do is come on my fingers. Can you do that and keep the bike up right?"

She doesn't say anything.

"Maggie?"

"I... I think so."

I know she turned on by the way her nipples are hard pebbles and the way she's rocking her hips against my cock.

My fingers slip under her yoga pants, touching a silk pair of panties. I cup her mound, applying pressure down on her center.

She moans.

"Keep your eyes open and on the road."

"You're making this driving lesson hard," she says with a little sexual frustration.

I laugh at her, knowing damn well I will have her coming undone on my fingers.

"You're a pro," my finger dips into her panties, sliding up her slit.

"Oh god," she cries out.

She's so fucking wet. Slipping my finger into her

wet heat, I massage her clit with my thumb. Fuck me she's soaking my hand, and I haven't even fucked her with my fingers yet. Sliding another finger into her, it stretches her.

A car passes by us honking its horn. I didn't realize we were going so slow, "Do the speed limit Pussycat."

Maggie comes out of her post sex haze enough to bring us up to the speed limit. When we're back alone on the road, I start moving my fingers in and out of her pussy as I keep up the movements against her clit. It doesn't take too long before Maggie starts breathing hard and rocking on the seat.

"Take what you need Pussycat, ride my fingers."

When she starts rocking on my fingers, her ass rubs my dick. I'm too painfully hard not to throw my head back from the sensation. Every rock forward I thrust my fingers into her hard. Hitting her clit with my thumb with each stroke.

"Fuck, you're going to make me cum in my pants. You dirty girl."

"Ohh, feels so good," her soft voice breathes out, whimpering in my ear.

Her pussy clenches around my fingers and I know she about to come.

"I'm about to—," she falls against my chest, and I grab the handlebars with my free hand as she screams out my name.

CHAPTER 25

Maggie

The distance closes as we come closer to the well kept grounds lined up around a white three-story house. It has the same breathtaking effect on me it did a few months ago. Stunning. The large wrap around porch is nothing short of a picture with the sun bouncing off the lake in the back yard.

My arms are wrapped around Colt's firm stomach. Every movement he makes, his abs contract and my hands find themselves exploring his stomach muscles a little more. The last time I let my hand wander he placed my hand over his hard cock, letting me know if I didn't stop, he was going to pull over and bend me over his motorcycle. I wasn't opposed to it, but I'm wanting to get there just to get off the two wheel death trap that's vibrating my clit into a horny frenzy. Between Colt's hard body and the amazing orgasm, he gave me earlier, I went into limp noodle mode and haven't quite recovered. That might be a hint as to why my driving lesson was short lived.

Colt doesn't stop at the garage like I expected him to do. Instead he drives around to the cute small building in the back.

Turning off the bike, I throw my leg over to climb off only to wobble when both feet are planted on the asphalt until Colt steadies me. He laughs a deep rumble that vibrates my insides. It's got to be the best music I've ever heard.

"Steady there, pussycat. I wouldn't want you to hurt yourself," he says, pulling me closer to his chest. "I've got all kind of plans for you this weekend. Having you bent over serving you my oversized cock is one of them," he whispers in my ear before he takes the lobe of it into his mouth. Biting me just enough to send a rushing heat flying though my body like a damn jet plane. This man!

Colt's face tilts, bringing his lips brushing over mine.

"Colt!" a voice yells.

"Mother fucker!" he says low enough for whoever not to hear him.

My eyes dart over to see Nat coming up to us. Fuck me! She's really starting to get on my nerves. I gave Charles to her on a silver platter, but I'd be fucking shit if I give up this one.

Quickly, Colt places a smile on his face when he sees Nat running up to us.

"What are you guys doing back here? Are you not

coming inside the house?" Nat asks Colt without acknowledging my existence.

Screw you too!

"We're going to get settled in first," he points to the small pool house.

I raise my eyebrows. Connie won't have us staying in the same room and if he's out here then I will have to be in there with her… by myself. Oh god. No. Please. No.

"Maggie and I are staying in the pool house," he says giving me what I needed to hear. "I've already told dad." He looks down as his eyes search mine.

I give him a small nod, thankful that he already planned ahead.

"Nat," he gets off his bike pulling her into a hug. "It was great to see you, but I need a shower and Maggie needs me to wash her back along with other parts of her body," he says winking at me.

She looks up at him fondly, "You two better find me after you get settled."

"Sure will," he kisses the top of her head and grabs our bags along with my hand and walks us to the poolhouse front door.

I turn to give Nat a wave expecting her to still have the same smile on her face. Instead, I find her with her arms crossed, stabbing me in the back with a knife so large it could easy make its way into Colt's large frame in front of me. Figure of speech of course, but I swear I can feel the intensity of a sharp edge slicing my insides.

I'm jerked in the pool house with lips attacking my neck. Colt slams the door with his foot, backing me up until my back hits the wall.

Greedy hands find my hips, "Turn around," he whips me around, not waiting on my compliance. "Bend over. I need to perform a cavity search... I'll be using a very large tool, so you'll need to brace yourself," his voice comes out husky and fuck me, a cavity search never sound so appealing.

Knock, knock.

"Fucking hell," Colt breathes out, holding his fingers still on the zipper of my pants. He lets out air, bringing his forehead to rest on my shoulder. "This will have to be delayed until a later time," he smacks my ass, pulling away and heading to the door.

Quickly I button my pants and try to calm my rushing hormones down. A horny Colt is something to behold and holding him in my mouth or in my pussy is something I'm always down with. The man is all male. Every. Last. Inch. By inch.

"Hey son!" Colt's dad sounds more than excited to see him. "Are you going to hold Maggie hostage in here all weekend, or you going to bring her in the house to see us?" his dad says as he pushes his way inside the small living space, walking over to me, he embraces me in a tight hug.

"Good to see you again, Maggie," his kind words give me a sense of home.

"Thank you, Mr. Donovan. Thank you for having me. I know things—" Colt's dad holds his hand up to stop me.

"No words are necessary Maggie. We all know Charles has his...flaws. I do know that my son here," he throws his arm around Colt's neck, pulling him into a head lock. "Is smitten with you but if he gets out of line, you come tell me." He gives Colt a quick noogie then lets him pull back. "Let's go inside the house, Connie has made lunch for everyone."

The sun beams down on us when we step outside, headed to the main house. It's quiet today, no boats are on the water, and it looks like all the neighbors are indoors. We walk through the back door and the aroma of food hits me in the face. The delicious smell of peppers, onions, and grilled seafood drift in the air making my stomach growl. I clutch my stomach, embarrassed that it was so loud.

"Take a seat," Connor says, pointing to a chair. "Connie went to go get freshened up," he looks around the family room like something is out of place. "Nat was here just a few minutes ago. She might have gone to see what Connie was up to. They'll be back soon, I'm sure," he suggests for us to pull out a chair.

On que, Nat strolls into the room wearing little to nothing. A small crop top with triangles covering her barely there boobs tie around her neck. The top is the most fabric she's wearing compared to the shorts. They barely cover her ass, which is hanging out under the hem.

Colt is already seated at the table and before I take a hold of the chair beside him Nat grabs it, planting her ass down into it.

"Maggie's sitting there," Colt's voice barks at Nat.

She blinks up at him. I don't know why but I feel bad for him snapping at her. I shouldn't feel bad because she should've known that was my seat.

"It's fine," Colt gives me a stern look. "Really. I'll sit across from you," I wrap my arms around his neck pushing my breasts in the back of his head. "I'll get to see your handsome face," I whisper in his hair.

He growls but doesn't say argue. *Good boy!*

When I take my seat his foot creeps up my leg, resting between my thighs. It makes me think how different Charles acted to Nat's flirting and close proximity. He was so wrapped up in her, he couldn't see out of the two eyes that rest on each side of his nose. The only vision that mattered to him was what he could see with his one eye monster.

"Connor—" Connie stops in the arch doorway leading into the kitchen and living space. Her face is of shock as she stares between me and Colt. Her eyes dart between us again then land on Connor. There's a quiet twitch in her left eye. It's barely noticeable, but I see a flash of irritation cross her face.

"Mag-gie," my name drips out of her mouth. "Charles isn't here. Should I... leave him a message?" she arches an eyebrow, waiting for me to respond.

This woman will be my undoing this weekend.

"She's with Colt," Connor says more nicely than she deserves.

She puffs out her chest, walking over to the table

and sets her fake ass down at one end of the table. I knew last visit I didn't like her, and she just confirmed I won't be changing my mind this visit, but for Colt and Connor's sake I need to try to get along with the old bat.

"Where is Charles?" I don't really want to know but I haven't seen him since Macy's wedding.

She peers up through her long-weaved eyelashes which I have no doubt that cost every bit of five hundred dollars.

"He's been busy," she looks down at her empty plate. "I'm not sure if he's going to make it this weekend." She looks to Nat, "Nat, glad you could join us," she comments a little too sweetly.

Interesting. Can't make it to his family's function but can crash a wedding.

"Dad, how are your sugar levels? Are you keeping a good check on it?" Colt questions his father.

While Colt makes small talk with his dad, I notice Connie doesn't have her normal resting bitch face on. She looks a bit... scared, when Colt mentions the hospital scare but is stopped midway in a sentence when Connie drops the plater of kebabs, causing them to spill out over the table.

She stands up trying to catch the food, setting it back on the platter one by one. Her hands are shaky making her not being able to drop the kebabs in the neat stack she original had them.

The hospital scare must have really shaken her up. I can't imagine her as a loving, doting wife but I could be wrong, or she could have tried to kill him and having second thoughts. I almost want to laugh at myself for thinking that. I watch way too much crime television but there have been crazier things women have done when it comes to a man.

She wouldn't, would she? What could be her motive? Money. It always leads back to the almighty dollar, but Connor said she saved him. No, she wouldn't. Connor would give her anything. This lake house is an example of that. It's screams expensive, luxury, and it's decorated just like a woman would have it, all pale colors, bright, and airy. There's nothing that man wouldn't do for the woman beside him. So why would she do it? Even if she did, how did she do it?

Nat and I help Connie gather the rest of the kebabs, then I place the platter in the middle of the table once we're finished. Connie quickly recovers trying to school her features, but it doesn't escape my attention that she looks like she's aged ten years since the beginning of our lunch. Her face is hard but is softer than it was an hour ago.

"Maggie, I'll show you where you will be staying after lunch," and there she is.

My eyes dart to Colt who's staring back at me. Silently I'm letting him know, he better break the news, or he can forget about giving me that cavity search.

"We'll be staying in the pool house," Colt voice is firm when he says it.

I stay silent, hoping this won't turn into a shit show. A clank vibrates the table, and we all turn to Nat who is staring at Colt with her mouth open.

She clears her throat, taking a bite out of the grilled shrimp. Her moan is loud when she closes her eyes tasting the flavor on her tongue.

The urge to slap that bite right out of her mouth is greater than wanting my next breath. This girl is a real slut puppy. When she opens her eyes, she makes contact with mine, there's a storm brewing in behind hers. An inkling falls over me that the destruction it'll bring will be with force of an F5 tornado.

CHAPTER 26

Maggie

Lunch was delicious and even if I hate to admit it, Connie is a great cook. I volunteer to clear the table to get in good graces with Colt's family, only to be out shined by Nat when she mentions bringing some desert her mother is famous for. Connie was more than thrilled to have her bring her mother's notorious desert. I couldn't help when my eyes rolled so far back into my head I saw my brain stem.

I set the dishwasher on the setting and press start when hands wrap my waist.

"Did you miss me?" a scratchy voice asks.

My body tenses. Nervously I pull myself away wanting to remove myself from the corner I'm trapped in.

"Ch…Charles?" It's more of a question than just stating his name.

Charles' hands drag across my stomach, then a

painful sound rings in the air. Charles is pinned under Colt as Colt delivers blows to Charles face. They start rolling on the floor with Charles trying to get out of Colt's grip but is unsuccessful.

"Colt!" I tug at his shirt trying to pull him off of Charles. "Stop it. Let him go,"

Nat stands at the end of the counter smirking giving me the evil eye.

Connor runs in from the back deck, commanding Colt to get off Charles but it doesn't stop him, he keeps delivering punches. I step back further out of the way. There's nothing I can do. Colt is larger than me and I would have to have the strength of ten men right now to pull him off Charles.

It doesn't take long for Connor to put Colt in a headlock. He yells at Charles to get up.

"Calm the hell down Colt," Connor says with his arm around his neck. "If I let you go, are you going to go after him again?" Colt's angry face doesn't hold back in letting us know he's not calmed down enough to be let loose.

Connor holds him until Colt has finally calmed down enough to be let go.

Colt points his finger at Charles. "Don't EVER fucking touch her again," Colt demands. He wraps his arm around my shoulders and tugs me to the back door.

"He didn't hurt you, did he?" Colts voice is much gentler than before.

"No. You shouldn't have done that. I was —"

Colt stops walking, turns me toward him. "No one touches what's mine!" His possessiveness floods off him, making the hairs on my neck stand up. Running his hand through his short dark hair, he lets out a breath. "He doesn't have a right to touch you. I mean what I say, you're mine Maggie. You were mine from the first moment I saw you. He fucked up and he knows it, but he doesn't get another chance. I branded you with my cock, there's no turning back."

If I thought I wanted Charles, Colt's aggressive behavior would have thrown the idea from my mind. There's nothing hotter like an angry Colt.

"Mr. Donovan," I slide my hands down his chest. "Does that get me out of that cavity search you promised me?" I bat my eyelashes.

He growls, lifting me up in the air over his shoulder he says, "Baby, I think you will need to be examine more closely and I've got just the right tool to do it."

***

My body feels better than a day at the spa. There's nothing like an afternoon of fucking then napping to gather your strength back.

My eyes are staring at the ceiling, and I'm trying to listen for any noise to tell me where Colt is in the small pool house. It's cute with it's one bedroom, a bath, living area. The kitchen is small but there's no use in having one since we will be eating at the main house, but it'll be nice at night if we want to heat any leftovers up.

The door closes and footsteps stop at the bedroom door.

"Are you still sleeping?"

"Hmm," I look over at Colt's half naked body, pulling myself up to my elbows as I lick my lips. This man is my walking wet dream. "Have you been up long?" I thought Colt had fallen asleep too, but I may have been the only one. He did a search that left me trembling with lack of energy.

"I couldn't sleep so I went for a swim," he walks over to me, bending at the knees as he kisses my forehead. "We're taking the boat out," his lips brush up against my ear. "You should have your strength back and I have plans for you to take my cock on the float."

I swat at his shoulder, making him laugh.

"I need a shower first, I smell like sex," I say, pulling the covers back as I start to get up.

"No," Colt's voice is deep. "I want everyone to smell me on you. I hope your pussy ate up every inch of my cum so that my scent will stay with you always."

Fuck me! That was the hot!

"Colt, as hot as that sounds. I smell like I've been rode hard."

The corners of his mouth pulls into a sinful grin, "That's because you did."

I laugh, walking into the bathroom. He's right, he did damage to my body that I'm definitely feeling. My muscles are sore, and I thought I was in fairly good shape, looks like I need to pick up a yoga class.

When I'm dressed, Colt's no longer in the bedroom so I walk out, stopping when I come into the living area. Nat is standing with her back against the front door.

"Nat what are you doing in here?" I look around for Colt. "Colt's not here."

There's really no where he could be. The pool house is only big enough to accommodate two people, maybe a small family.

"Oh no, he told me to come and get you," she says looking at her nails.

I need to tread lightly around her. She's sending me signals that she might not have all her marbles upstairs.

"They've got the boat ready to head out," she looks up at me and smiles.

Yeah, it's not a friendly smile. It's more like something out of a horror movie.

"I'm ready," I take a step towards the front door to open it, but Nat doesn't move.

"Listen," she puts her hand up to stop me. "I just wanted to say I feel really bad about Charles. I was at a place in my life that I didn't like myself and didn't care what damage I caused with friends and family," she holds out her hand in a truce.

Hesitantly I shake it waiting to get stabbed in the process but the smile she puts on makes me relax. Maybe, I was wrong about her. Maybe, she's not at all crazy.

"And I just want you to know, Colt is a dear friend of mine and if you so much as hurt him, I'll cut your throat. Just saying," she bounces in place before she grabs the door handle, opening it as she leaves me standing with my mouth open.

Nope, she's still crazy!

My phone rings in my bag and I fish for it hoping I can grab it before it goes to voicemail. The ring tone is set to my sister's favorite song, so I know it's her calling.

"You are never going to believe this?" my sister whispers on the phone.

"Jessica, what's wrong?" my voice comes out in a rush.

"Guess who got arrested?" she snickers into the phone.

"Do not tell me you, mom, or dad. I would literally die," I comment. I doubt any of them would get arrested for anything especially my parents they live a boring life. No real excitement has happened in their life since the eighties.

"Fuck no. Could you imagine if dad was arrested? Mom would be having a baby calf."

"Then who?" there isn't anyone that I kept up with other than Macy and I've not spoken to her in bits and pieces since they got back from their honeymoon. They're still trying to get everything sorted from the wedding.

"Charles!" her voice screams into the phone.

Speaking of the devil, Charles opens the back door

of the house. Stepping out he meets my gaze. He still looks so unkept, so unlike the Charles I knew. His hair is longer with the facial hair that is unruly on his face. He's skinner than I remember plus the bruises that he's now sporting from Colt's fist.

"Maggie, are you still there?"

I shut the door to the pool house not wanting anyone to hear me, "Charles is here," I whisper just in case someone walks by. "He can't be in jail, he's here Jess."

"The old mother hen could have bailed him out."

That's true.

Colt opens the door, "You ready?" his eyes roam my body. "Oh Maggie, that bathing suit," he adjusts himself. "Baby, I'm going to make my fantasies come true tonight," he smirks.

"Jessica, I have to go. I'll call you later."

"Don't forget about this Sunday," she yells as I hang up the phone. I forgot about brunch with my parents. I hope Colt doesn't mind cutting our weekend early. I've not seen my mom and dad in weeks. That's not normal for me. I usually make time out every other week to go and have breakfast with them.

Colt holds a hand out to me, "Let's go Pussycat."

Once we've boarded the pontoon, I sat down in the corner of the bench thinking of what my sister just had blew my mind with, Charles was arrested. I didn't even have time to ask her why, or how she found out.

I'm so completely lost in thought of all the reasons

why he was in jail that I don't notice Nat when she sits down beside me, breathing over my shoulder. Why is she so clingy all of a sudden?

My phone chimes and I pick it up to see a text from an unknown number.

I'm watching you, make sure to wear a life jacket. People drown all the time.

I scream out, dropping my phone like it has the plague. Jumping up from my seat I dart off the boat, leaving all my belongings on the boat. I don't stop running until I make it inside of the small pool house. Rushing to the bedroom, I yank my bag out of the closet and start stuffing everything in. Colt runs in after me, grabbing my shoulders and pulling me up against him.

"Maggie, what happened?" his voice is full of concern. "Turn around and look at me," he pleads.

I shake my head, not able to look at him.

"Please talk to me," he pleads again.

There hasn't been any more attempts of getting chased, no fuck up messages, so why now? Why this weekend? Is it someone here, could it be Charles? My mind is going through all the scenarios of who it could be and why would they choose me.

My eyes burn with tears as I fight to keep them from escaping. I need to get mad. I need to let whoever this person is know I won't be so easily scared but the fact is… I am. I'm scared of not being strong enough to fight this fear inside of me because if I want to keep Colt and to stay, I need to face this head on and push

this fear away. I need to overcome this want to run. If
I don't then I'll lose and that means whoever this is
will win.

CHAPTER 27

Colt

Maggie's scream filled my body with adrenaline, kicking me into protective mode. My heart raced with bolts of lightning striking it, with every bit of the force trying to bring me to my knees. If it wasn't for my brain knowing exactly what I needed to do, I wouldn't have known to chase after her.

Her knees are drawn up against her as she lies curled up in my arms. She willingly came back to the boat without much coaching on my behalf. I'm thankful for her deciding to rejoin us, but she didn't want to tell me why she ran. I could guess or snoop, but I would rather have her tell me what made her react that way. If she doesn't tell me, I'll wait until she goes to sleep tonight to browse through her phone. I know it has to be something that was related to her phone, because when she screamed it flew out of her hands, landing on the boat. Only when we got back it was in her bag, making me wonder why someone would put it there, but I intend on asking dad who put it in her bag and placed it on her seat.

The only person that even seemed concerned when we returned to the boat was my dad. Which shouldn't surprise me. He's the only one with a heart. Nat looked like the Cheshire cat winning a grand prize. It surprises and pisses me off she's taking pleasure from Maggie's pain. Then there's Charles and Connie who didn't budge from their seats. Their stuck-up asses stayed seated the entire time, at least Nat made some of show to act concern about Maggie when I returned with Maggie in my arms.

Charles and I haven't spoken since our fight. He's not even looked at me once today. There's no love lost on my half. I've never liked him to begin with. I did used to care years ago. I tried to be his friend until one day when he made the comment about why my mother was taken away from me.

You're a loser Colt. No wonder your mother died, she couldn't stand the thought of having you for a son.

I couldn't force myself to even try to be his friend. All his jealously kept getting in the way of us being close. So I stopped trying. Then things got worse with Connie after I stop kissing Charles' ass. They came into my dad's house trying to be better than me. Trying to take everything I loved away from me. My mother's memory, anything she gave me, and my dad. Only their plan didn't work on my dad like they had hoped. Our bond is tight.

"Colt," my dad's voice is muffled by the wind as the boat sails on the water. "Do you and Maggie want to ride on the float?" he grins at me.

Fucker!

I know he saw me finger Maggie the last time we were here. He's not said anything to me about it, but he's always bringing the ride up like he trying to coax it out of me. Sometimes I tell him about the girls I'm with, like I said we have a close bond, but Maggie is not a whore and I'm not telling a soul about her pussy. He can keep guessing, I'll never tell.

"You feel like getting on the float?" I whisper in her ear.

She shakes her head.

I had a feeling she wouldn't. She's still trembling in my arms.

"I'll ride with you Colt," Nat says, making my skin itch at the thought of having to be that close to her. In the past I didn't mind when we would pair up but after today, something just doesn't settle with me being on the float with her.

"No. I think I'll stay here with Maggie."

"Go. Have fun," Maggie's voice is weak.

I try to protest but Maggie's insistent with demanding I have fun. The thought of Nat being so close to me on the float doesn't sit well, but there's no way to let Maggie know without being so loud that everyone will hear me.

I give in after dad tells me he'll watch Maggie.

Slowly rising up, I place a kiss on her lips, "It'll be

223

a short ride. Save my seat," letting my eyes roam to Charles and Connie when I finally stand. Connie has her sunglasses on, blocking what she's actually looking at, and Charles has a distant stare on his face looking into the water.

Nat's waiting for me on the ledge to jump off onto the float.

"Can you help me?" she asks a little too sweetly for me.

I give her a push into the water causing her to scream. Chuckling, I plunge into the water.

When we're on the float I give dad the signal to take off. It's smooth sailing when he starts the boat in drive, and I stretch my neck up looking like a damn turtle trying to catch a glimpse of Maggie. Caught by surprise when Nat's hand swats my ass, then grabs my shorts pulling them down a bit.

"Fucking hell Nat," I snarl, jerking my head to her. She lets out a slight scream from losing her balance.

Doing my best to help her I pull her upright in the middle of the float with my hand wrapped around her middle. My body is hovering over her, trying to hold her in place from falling again.

"You got it?" I ask when her hands and feet are safety back on the ropes.

"Yes," she responds back while brushing her ass up against me.

I freeze in place. Never expecting Nat to act that way. When she looks up to me and smiles, I let go of the ropes that's I'm holding onto and fall back in the water. I knew she had a crush on me growing up, but never thought much more of it. I was too focused on giving Charles hell for lusting after her like a little sick puppy. Maybe, it nothing. Maybe, it was just her getting her body in a better position so she wouldn't fall off. Whether it was or not, I didn't feel comfortable with her trying to rub my dick.

Dad comes back around, and I opt to climb back into the boat rather than on the float with the she devil. Maggie hands me a towel when I grab my seat, then snuggles back into my side. My muscles relax from the strain they felt when Nat was up against my skin. This is how it's supposed to feel—natural.

Not long after I climb into the boat, dad doesn't get down the lake too far when Nat falls off. I can't say that it wasn't on purpose. She might have thought I would have gone in after her when she flopped around splashing water as if she was going to down with a life jacket on. She didn't think her act through when I yelled out to her about having it on.

We've been riding the water in silence since. There's a great deal of tension in the air, nothing like it was the last time we were all together. Everyone is sitting with a blank look on their face. If it wasn't for my dad wanting us to come up, I would have much rather stayed at home curled up with a naked Maggie beside me this weekend.

It's dark outside when we finally pull up at the dock.

"Colt, hop off tie off the boat."

Everyone piles off and Maggie is the next to last to exit. I steal a kiss before letting her go. Fuck this woman does all kinds of things to my mind. She continues to walk up the dock. She still doesn't seem like herself, so I have a plan to loosen her up the best way I know how. Running up behind Maggie, I sweep her up into my arms. Her laughter filters in my ears like a beautiful lullaby.

"Throw your bag down baby," my voice is filled with mischief.

"What? Why? Colt Donovan what are you planning?" her eyes narrow at me.

I keep running to the pool, "Throw it down or get it wet. One way or the other I don't care."

Before I make it to the edge to jump in, she throws her bag over to the lounge chair, but it misses when it lands on the concrete with a thump. Just in time before I submerge us under the water. She doesn't fight me under water when I raise her bottles to place each hand on a bare ass cheek. I grind her front up against me, letting her feel how hard I am. When we come back up for air, the back door shuts.

"Colt," her voice comes out with a bit of anger but I can see in her eyes it's playful.

"Mag-gie," I mock her.

I pull her legs up, wrapping them around my waist, "Have you ever been fucked in a pool?" my nose skims down her neck, making goosebumps rise up.

"No," her voice is filled with want.

"Then you'll need to be quiet when I fill you with

my cock," I say, swimming us to the edge that is closest to the back door. The height of the pool walls block anyone inside from seeing us. "Pull me out pussycat," her hand snakes its way into my shorts, wrapping around my cock, making my dick harder.

"Fuck," I grunt. "How does even your hand feel so damn good?"

My fingers brush up against her pussy and I push the thin strap of material to the side. Exposing her to me. I line myself up as I give a hard thrust, letting the water ripples crash into our faces. Her moans fill the air. Maggie's head rolls back against the wall. She looks more at ease than she has all day.

She grinds her sweetness against me, making me close my eyes savoring the moment. When I tilt my head back, I thank the heavens for this woman. Opening my eyes, they collide with Charles who peering down from the second floor window watching us. A vicious plan forms in my mind to let the fucker watch. I know he's not able to make out anything but our silhouette. It's pitch black out tonight, no lights are on that surround the pool or any lights from inside the house. But I can't. I know Maggie wouldn't forgive me if I did.

I pull back from Maggie, she whimpers, opening her eyes she questions me, "Something wrong?"

"We've got an audience," I say, directing my eyes to the second floor.

"Shit," she mumbles when she sees Charles still staring.

"We could keep going... if you want to put on a show for him," I suggest. I'm not keen on the idea of him seeing or hearing her cries when I give her an orgasm, but I'll do anything Maggie wants if it means making her happy.

"No...I want to go inside," the softness of her voice lets me know she's not into making him jealous. Good. I offered, but the last thing I want to give Charles is something to jerk off to later.

I leap up using my arms to turn myself over the edge and stand up. I take her hands and help her out and we head to the pool house scooping up her bag on our way.

***

The next morning, I wake up before Maggie and head into the main house to grab a little breakfast. It's still pretty early, so I'm not expecting anyone up when I shut the door behind me.

Connie jumps when I shut the door.

"Colt," her hand flies to her chest. "You... scared me. I wasn't expecting anyone to be up this early."

I frown. She looks awfully suspicious with her arms down her side.

"What are you making?" the halves of a grapefruit lay in front of her.

"Nothing...just preparing a meal for your Dad. You know he's not allowed to eat certain foods now, so I'm making sure he's eating healthier," her explanation is rushed.

The hairs on my arms stand up. I want to write it

off but there's something wrong with her body language, she's stiff and her eyes don't may contact with mine. What is she hiding behind her? I stand watching what's she's going to do next, but she doesn't move. Still standing with a guilty gleam in her eye, she waits on me to leave. Only I don't plan on leaving until I find out what she's up to.

Fear flashes in her catlike eyes when I move closer to the counter. Eagerly waiting on her next move, I wait patiently as I slow my steps. My hand lands on the corner counter-top, swinging myself around to see what's she's hiding. Her arm jerks up with a syringe and tries to stab me in the hand, but I react faster moving it away.

"Don't come any closer," she threatens me with the needle aimed in the air.

"Connie, just set the needle down," I say, holding my hands up in the air.

She takes a few calculated steps backwards.

I know she's going to run for it. I need to engage her in a conversation loud enough where someone would wake up and come to help, preferably not Charles. He would take her side rather than help retain her.

"Connie," I need to reason with her. "Whatever that is can't be worth ruining your life over."

Gently I take a step toward her, only to have her step back one. The back door opens, drawing Connie's attention draw to it. I leap forward to take action, but a sharpness strikes my shoulder. Connie's gasp echoes though the quiet house.

"Oh god!" she screams out. Her hands are drawn to her face covering her mouth then sliding up her face and into her hair. I feel slightly lightheaded, reaching out I brace myself against the countertop. Voices are like white noise growing fainter in the background.

I need to rest.

"Here," Connie's voice screams into my ear.

My eyes open wide trying to stay focus on Maggie's face as I fall to the floor. Someone moves my head and there's a softness placed under my head.

"Colt I'm going to place this jelly in your mouth," Connie's voice booms.

I feel cold shaky fingers tremble when my lip is pulled down and a sweetness is placed between my lip and gums. It doesn't take long until I'm able to get my bearings on my surroundings. My breathing is still a bit shaken, wondering what was in that syringe.

Maggie's breath fans across my face, and I take in the comfort of her embrace. My head is resting on her thighs with her hand stroking my hair.

Connie is standing over us with her hands rubbing her chest as if she's the one in pain.

"What the hell is all the commotion down here?" Dad asks.

Maggie and I both look to Connie to start explaining. She meets our eyes, bouncing back and forth between us pleading, begging for us not to say anything. She has to know I would never choose her over my dad.

"Connie has something she needs to tell all of us," Maggie and dad help me up out of the floor to a chair at the kitchen table.

"Connie, I'm waiting. Do you have a good reason why Colt was laying on the floor and his color is pale like he was about to die?" he places his hands on his hips. That's his stance when he doesn't want to hear any bullshit.

Charles comes rushing down the stairs into the kitchen, looking all ruffled up. He doesn't ask questions and he doesn't look at anyone when he walks to the refrigerator to grab the orange juice. Does he know what Connie was up to?

"Charles, do you know what your mother was doing with this needle?" I raise it up for him. I pulled it out but kept it in my hand in case she tried to stab me again.

"No idea," he comments as if he's seen this all played out before.

"You need to start explaining," my dad's voice is gruff.

She shakes her head not being able to find her voice.

"Get out! Get out of my house. If you are up to no good and clearly you have been."

"Noo, Connor please!" she begs. "I just ... you needed... I needed you to know how much you needed me," her face looks painful, stricken with hurt.

"What?" my dad's voice is softer. "Connie what

have you done?" he shakes his head, running his fingers through his hair, blowing out a breath. "This is all my fault. I shouldn't have showered you with whatever you wanted. I gave you too much,"

"Please," she begs. "I just needed to show you needed me to take care of you. What happened to Colt was an accident," she sniffles like it's going to save her. Her eyes cast down when she speaks, "The amount of insulin was very little," my dad's eyes go wide.

He's being having black out moments thinking Connie was helping him, but she's been the one that's been causing the harm to his body. Then manipulating him to into thinking she was a saint so keeps her around, all because she didn't want to lose his money. Everything makes perfect sense now. He's not been able to control his diabetes because she's been toying with it. Connie was a nurse when they met. She knew exactly how much to give not to kill him and that's how she knew to put the jelly on the inside of my lip.

"Get out," Dad says, pointing his finger at her. "Charles, go get your mother's purse. She'll be leaving now," his attention falls back to Connie. "How could you? You could have killed me... or Colt," Charles comes back with her purse, putting it in dad's hand. "Leave Connie, I don't ever want to see you again. I'll send your things later." He digs in her purse, pulling out her keys then takes off a key and hands them over to her.

She drops her head and tears cover her hands but they can't save her. She made this mess for herself. He grabs her forearm and rushes her out into the garage. When the door glides up and the light shines through the door opening, Maggie takes in a sharp intake of air.

"She's leaving, you won't have to worry about her anymore," I say, smirking with a good riddance salute to Connie as dad hauls her off by the arm.

"Her car is green?" Maggie whispers.

CHAPTER 28

Maggie

My world is spinning, taking in the green sedan
Connie is climbing into. I can't be certain that it's the
same car that tried to run me over, but the color is
close enough to give me shivers. I didn't tell Colt

Connie's spirit looks broken as she begs Connor to
listen to her. A string tugs at my heart. I hate to see a
family broken but somehow, I don't think they were a
family. I think Connie liked the idea of coming across
as a picture-perfect couple, but never a loving family.
A warm hand slips into mine. His large hands covered
with callus holds my hand so tenderly.

"Are you staying?" I ask Charles. A part of me
hopes he'll leave.

His eyes don't even flinch when I ask my question.
I find it fascinating how he's able to stay so calm
during the showdown. Why wouldn't he be upset at
Connor kicking his own mother out? Maybe, Charles

has his own set of problems that no one knows about. Maybe he's immune to his mother's crazy ways, or maybe he's just wanting to hang around enough to end my life or Colts. Charles stares at me, giving me the creeps.

The way he was fixated on us last night in the pool. I wasn't even at ease when the pool house door shut, and we were safely tucked away from his eyes. I wouldn't let Colt turn the light on for fear of Charles making out where we were in the room, so I pulled him into the shower. The bathroom is the only room in the small house that doesn't have windows besides the closets.

Connor closes the door, blocking out the light of hope this day would turn out to be normal.

"Charles it's time we have a family meeting. Sit down," he says in a nonsense voice.

We all take a seat around the large breakfast table before Connor starts to talk.

"Charles, you're still a part of this family," he points between him and Colt. "Unless you don't want to be or… if you do something to screw it up," he sits, waiting on Charles to say something. "There will be no more free rides. No more money being handed down to you. I won't cut you off, but there will not be an endless amount of money to be given to you when you expect it. If you agree, you're always welcome here but if you think I won't bring charges up against you if I find you stealing or anything you shouldn't be doing you, will be wrong. Do I make myself clear?"

Connor eyes bore into Charles.

Charles swallows, raising his eyes up to meet Connor. He glances over to me and Colt. I try not to stare feeling like I shouldn't be here during this conversation.

"I understand," Charles' voice is weak.

The atmosphere has become filled with a suddenly strange feeling. I decide to head back to the pool house. I was hoping to take a moment and ask Colt if we could leave early today to head to my parents' house but with everything that happened today, I'm not sure if that would be a great idea. His dad may need him.

"I'm going to go and clean up a little," I announce, raising up.

Before I turn the knob to the small pool house, Colt reaches me, "Do you have anything in mind you want to do today?"

"I wanted to talk to you about that," I push the door open, walking over to the small couch. "My parents are having brunch tomorrow. I wanted to see if we could leave early to stay with them a night. Just so you know, my parents are still very old fashioned and we won't be able to share a room."

He lifts his lip up, "Let's just head back, we can leave in the morning to go to your parents' then come back tomorrow night. I don't want to be without you in my bed."

I agree. There's nothing like waking up with his long arms around me.

"Does your dad need you to be here?" I want to be considerate but really, I just want to bail. I'm over this day.

Colt leaves to go find his dad and I start packing when a knock occurs. I locked the door when Colt left, scared of someone coming in on me when I wasn't paying attention. Connie could come back with a vengeful attitude. I don't want to be on the receiving end of her rampage.

The sheer curtain covering the window doesn't provide privacy inside the house. Charles is standing with his nose pressed against the window, looking in. There's no need for ducking down or trying to hide because he gives me a small wave when he sees me walking out the bedroom. I plaster a smile on my face, not wanting to deal with whatever crap he wanting to dish out.

If he tries to touch me, I'm going to deck him.

"Hey, are you looking for Colt? Because he went to go find Connor," I stand in the doorway to block him from trying to come in.

"No, I wanted to talk to you. Do you have a minute?" he steps closer, looking to be invited in.

Stepping in the doorway I pull the door behind me. If he's wanting to talk to me then I need to make sure it's somewhere people can hear me if I need to scream. I don't want to take a chance of getting cornered if he makes a move.

"Right here will be fine," I give him my best let's get to the point look.

His face falls at me being harsh, "I... I need to apologize for the way I've been acting."

I stare at him, not even blinking. This is not the Charles that I know. The one I knew would never apologize to anyone. What's changed with him to make him want to say sorry?

"I've been…" he inhales a deep breath. "I got…" he shakes his head, "I picked up a drug habit."

My jaw drops. Could that be why he started acting so strange while we dated?

"I know it doesn't excuse the way I acted with you, but everyone acts different and hides it in their own way. I'm in counselling now thanks to Connor," he waits on me to comment.

"I'm sorry to hear that," I really am. I had no ideal and if I did, I would've supported him in getting the help he needed. "That doesn't excuse you for sleeping with Nat and saying I was beneath you, but it does explain how disheveled you looked when you showed up at Macy's wedding."

"Sleeping with Nat was like a childhood dream," he laughs but it doesn't sound like there's amusement in it. "But it ended up being a mistake especially since she dumped me afterwards. Anyway, it took me getting arrested to come to terms with the drug use. I don't want to be that person. I don't want my life to go down the shitter," his face contorts with pain.

Curious if I drove him into doing drugs I ask, "Was it because of me you started using drugs?"

His brows form a sharp V, and he reaches his

hands up to my shoulders but drops them, "No, not at all. I was trying to climb that corporate ladder. I needed to get all my work done and I was trying to work ten times harder than anyone else. Speed helped to keep me up at night, to push me though the work load I was volunteering for. One thing led to another then I started using them along with buying prescriptions from people all the time just to keep going when I wasn't working."

Relief fills me, "I'm glad you're getting help."

"This thing between you and Colt..." he fumbles around, kicking his flip flop on the concrete patio. "Is it serious?"

Is it serious?

I don't know how to answer that. I think we are. But until we have that talk of marriage, babies, and a white picket fence I definitely don't think I should be telling Charles about my feelings for Colt. I haven't even told him how much I care, maybe even love him. I answer him with the best answer I would give to any acquaintance.

"We're only dating each other," he looks at me to explain more, but that's the only answer I'll allow myself to give him. He doesn't need to know more, not since I don't even know where we stand.

Someone clears their throat behind Charles. Poking my head around Charles shoulders I see Colt. His stance is overpowering, legs spread, shoulders back, and chest out with his arms folded. He looks every bit like the terminator ready to pounce.

"Well, I need to go. I've got to help Connor get everything ready for the winter. We're leaving today, seems like mom killed it for everyone," he leans down to kiss my cheek, but a growl from Colt makes him snap his back straight, thinking better of it.

Colt shoots Charles a death glare when he walks off and I mouth to him to behave before I turn back to go finish packing.

My backpack sits on the bed where I left it, and I stuff the last of my clothes into it. I packed Colt's bag for him, but I ask him to check to make sure I didn't leave anything out. It's still a long trip out here just to have to come back. We search all the common areas, satisfied we've got everything packed. As soon as I've stripped the sheets, washed the dishes, and cleaned up any mess that was in the living space, we're headed out side.

"I've already told dad we're leaving," Colt says, locking the door to the small house.

Words fall out of my mouth before I can stop them, "Why do you think Charles didn't defend his mother when your dad kicked her out? Don't you find that a little strange?"

He pulls back slowly to look down at me, "Connie apparently wasn't as great as a mother to him as we thought, from what dad told me." He keeps talking as he guides me to his motorcycle. "I've always had it in my head that she took from me to give to him, but it wasn't true. The reason why he was so jealous of me was because she didn't give him what he really wanted, her love. Plus dad explained the trouble he's been into and feels bad for him so he's helping him out with his problem," he takes my backpack strapping it down on the back of the bike.

"You want to drive?" He wiggles his eyebrows," with a smile spreading from cheek to cheek.

I laugh at how naughty he is, "No, you drive, I'm going to enjoy the scenery."

My butt sits on the leather cushion, burning though my jeans from the sun's hot rays. We pull up to the end of the drive-way when a green sedan with limo tint creeps by, leaving me in an uncomfortable state. My hold on Colt because more of a death grip.

He speaks into the mic of the helmet, "What's wrong?"

"That sedan, it's green just like Connies, just like the one that tried to run me down."

The bike jumps forward, "Hold on… tight," Colt's voice is hard.

Oh god please don't let me die today. Please.

The Harley races down the road and the green car picks up speed. I have a death grip on Colt's waist, my head is turned resting on his back, and a silent prayer muttering from my lips.

No way can that car out run this bike. Whoever is driving must come to the same conclusion because they pull into a gas station and park a few spots down from the door. Colt cuts the corner a little too sharp, any closer to the pavement and I would eat gravel.

The pipes from the bike echo off the tin roof over

the gas pumps when he drives through them and comes to a stop beside the sedan, kicking his kickstand down not turning it off, he jumps off the bike. The door flies open and Charles steps out.

CHAPTER 29

Colt

My foot kicks the kickstand down with force and I jump off my bike taking two long strides over to the car. The door opens before I can pull it off the hinges and Charles steps out with a surprised look on his face.

Fucker!

"What the hell Charles?" I look at the car, trying to inspect it. "When did you get this?" I point to the car. It was only a few months ago I saw him drive a white midsize car.

"Purchased it last week. Why?" he looks over at my bike. "It sat out in the driveway. I'm surprised you didn't see it," he comments while playing innocent.

He's right. If he was trying to hide it. I wouldn't have seen it.

"Why did you run when you knew I was trying

to catch up with you?"

"Had no idea you were behind me. I'm a fast driver, ask Maggie," his body language doesn't come across as being an ass. The Charles we have all grown to know would make statements that would piss anyone off, but not this time. He's too calm never losing eye contact when he talks. There's not even a twitch in his eye which is always the sign he's lying.

I lower my visor and hop back on the bike, giving him a slight wave. I'm not ready to dismiss him from being a suspect but I'll give him a benefit of a doubt for now. My phone vibrates in my pocket when we start to pull out of the gas station parking lot. Two small vibrations let me know it's a text. I can't pull over because the traffic in the lot is crazy busy, so I'll wait until I get to Maggie's.

The ride back is long. It's the same distance we traveled to the lake house, but it seems longer headed home. There's nothing like wanting to get home and crawl in the bed after a long hot shower with my woman beside me. My woman. I smile to myself loving the sound of that. Maggie is my woman. She was from the moment I saw those long legs. I reach back and rub her thigh enjoying having this beautiful creature on the back of my bike.

"Go below," Maggie says in our builtin mics.

Slowly I turn the corner to make my way down the ramp to the underground parking deck. I shouldn't have been so careless with her on my bike earlier today. If I had hit someone or been hit, I couldn't have lived with myself. She's the last person that I would want to get hurt and especially if I was at fault for being so careless.

I pull up to the gate, "Do you have your badge?" she swipes a card, and the arm raises up for me to enter.

There's an empty space beside her car and I pull into it, turning the bike off. Maggie swings her leg over, standing a little unsteady.

"Woah there pussycat, take it easy. You're not use to riding long distances," smiling at her, I wink.

She rolls her eyes at me. Lucky for her my phone rings distracting me from hauling her over my knee. Cutters name flashes on the screen.

"Yeah," I wait for him to speak. He never calls when he knows I'm at my dad's.

"You need to get to the clubhouse," his voice is urgent.

"On my way," I hang up and slide my hand around Maggie, pulling her closer to me. Reaching up with the other hand I slide it into her hair, pulling her face down to kiss her. I take my time enjoying her lips on mine. The way her tongue melts with mine like two souls coming together. I don't want to stop but I know I need to head out to help with whatever problem it is at the club house.

Maggie sucks in my bottom lip and I almost come in my pants.

"Did you enjoy that?" she asks in a sultry voice.

"You have my cock's full attention," grabbing her

hand I place it on my aching groin. "I have to leave to take care of business, but I'll be back. I won't be able to sleep anymore without you being in my bed."

A smile tugs at the corners of my mouth. I have to force myself to start the bike to ride off, cursing Cutter as I head to the clubhouse.

Minutes later I pull up at the clubhouse, a small light shines through the house. When I walk inside Cutter, Jay, Shadow, and J-Bird are gathered around in the living room. They're all nursing a drink, looking casual as hell. I left my woman to meet up with these fuckers for a drink?

I point to Cutter, "You," he doesn't put on his normal joker face. "What's this about?" I stand crossing my arms, preparing myself for some serious shit.

***

"You're fucking kidding me?" I punch the wall knocking a hole in it. There's something else I'll have to fix or replace.

"What do you want to do about it? It's your call," J-Bird tells me.

I've just found out who destroyed my bar. I have a gut instinct they're the one that chased Maggie down, but there's two problems. They don't own a green car and I have no way of proving it. I need to think about how I'm going to get a confession.

"You could always beat it out of them?" Shadow casually says. He has no problem with giving male or female a bullet between the eyes.

CHAPTER 30

Maggie

It's been days since we got back from Colt's dads. We've in a nightly routine or I could say mid-morning routine when he comes to my apartment. Shower first, sex, and cuddling which ends with him spooning me. I couldn't have ever thought I would be happier with a younger man. I've always thought an older man would take care of me better, but I was wrong. Colt has shown me how wrong I was for dismissing younger guys. He pays attention when I talk, engaging in the conversation with feedback, tells me I'm beautiful and usually ends up with saying how great he thinks my breasts are.

Last night at dinner, Colt told me for the first time he loved me. The way his eyes sparkled when he said it, I was on top of the world. Then he got down on one knee and my mouth went dry. We haven't been dating long, but my heart raced waiting for him to say something, anything. When he brought his hand up holding his fork, I busted out laughing. People stared but I couldn't have cared less. I grabbed him by the ears, drawing him closer to kiss. It was one of the hottest fucking things I've ever done. My name can stay Ms. Or Mrs. in front of it. All I care about is spending my days and nights in his arms forever.

The weather is getting cooler outside. Fall popped up a little quicker this year. My hair is in a high ponytail since it's my day not to wash it I opt in putting it up, leaving my neck exposed to the cooler air. I pull out my favorite blue scarf and wrap it around my neck. The scarf will help stop from getting chills. Sometimes it gets cooler in the back office. I'm guessing from the lack of body heat until Colt shows up, pretending he needs to go over the inventory list.

Assessing myself, I take in my outfit. The baby blue floral pattern brings out the color in my eyes. Colt always complements my eyes, saying they're one of many of my best features. I swear that man could sell white gloves to a coal miner.

On the way out of my apartment I pick up my hand bag and keys, ready to go. I've been working for Colt longer than I had thought I would. Mr. Kung who was supposed to be my next client said he had hired someone full time and didn't need me any longer. He barely let me speak when he rushed the words out, then hung up on me when I was mid-sentence. When I told Colt about it, he offered me a position full time. I'm still not sure if I'll take it, but the steady work is something I can value. It's good to know I have a steady check coming in with the cost of living that is never ending on the rising side.

There's not but a handful of cars in the parking lot when I pull in and drive around the back of The Mule. I gather my things from the passenger side, open my door, and scream. My hand lays flat against my chest holding my racing heart from busting out of my chest.

"Shit, you scared the crap out of me," I bend over to pick up my purse when something hits me in the back of my head. I close my eyes squeezing them shut with pain shooting though me. When I open my eyes, specks of wet flakes drip up from my eyelashes. I can't tell the color just that whatever it is. It's dark. That's when everything fades to black.

CHAPTER 31

Colt

Seated in my office I keep my eyes on the screem. My
hands are balled into fists ready to rip someone apart.
I was a fool. How could I be so blind? I release my fist
trying to relax but there's no need, I can't. Standing
up, I pace the floor waiting to hear the word that they
found her. My anger is past boiling, it's red hot lava
ready to erupt, destroying anything in its path. My
phone beeps it's a text. I say a silent prayer.

Please let them find her.

I've been on edge since the day I came back from
my weekend with Maggie, patiently waiting,
wondering when something will happen. When I was
told what was planned, I couldn't restrain the
enraged motions. I didn't go back to Maggie's that
night. I was too drunk, too upset over what my ears
burned from hearing. My brothers have my back
that's for certain. Always looking out for me and my

best interests. I'll never be able to repay them.

Now here I stand, another day of waiting. I snatch the phone up, ready to have answer.

Shadow: Check your screen. She's pulling into the parking lot.

Shadow and Cutter have been working together to catch her in the act and today may just be the day. I leap into my chair. Almost falling out of it from the force of my weight putting pressure on the old thing. It's not the best of chairs. I make a mental note to order a new one or pick one up at the local office supply store.

The small screen shows Maggie's car pulling around the back and parking in her normal parking space. It's always the far corner away from the entrance. I could tell her a thousand times to stop parking in that dark corner, but she doesn't listen. I need to put the dumpster in that spot just to keep her ass from doing it. That'll be next on my list.

Maggie gathers items from the passenger side and opens the door and then… it happens. My seat flies behind me but I don't have time to worry if it went through the wall. I have to get to Maggie.

Shadow and Cutter have the perv in a tight grip, planting their face into the paint of Maggie's car.

"Maggie," I scream out.

She's not moving. Jay is on his phone standing in the open car door and I shove him back.

"Maggie, baby," I check for vital signs. "Thank you," I say silently when I feel her heartbeat.

There's blood streaming down the top of her head. Without wasting time, I pull my shirt off and place it on her head. I don't have time to worry about the perpetrator, I need to get Maggie to the hospital, lifting her up I gently move her over to the passenger side.

"I'm taking her to the hospital," I slam the door shut, rolling the window down to hear Jay.

He hangs up the phone, "I was calling an ambulance. I'm coming with you," he says, climbing into the backseat like a true friend. He yells, "What the fuck are you waiting for? Go, go, go."

When Jay's large hand wraps around Maggie's neck, I want to bark and snarl, but I suppress my jealous feelings. I know my friend is just helping her. He keeps my shirt placed on top of Maggie's head, making sure she doesn't lose too much blood. There's blood splatter on the steering wheel, windshield, and down her shirt. Her face is pale, worrying me that she's not going to make it. I can't lose her. I just can't. She's my everything. My need to breathe. My need to exist.

I come to abrupt stop at the emergency entrance, vaulting out the door and running around to pull her out.

"Park the car," I bark off to Jay as I scoop Maggie up, sprinting into the lobby.

The same lady sits at the desk from when I was here last. She looks up at me again with wide eyes. Only this time, it's from the look I'm giving her. I don't have time to fill out papers and if she asks me to, I can't be held responsible for what I say or do to her.

She jumps off the chair she perched on and yells something out. The automatic doors open, and she yells out for me to follow her. Maggie hasn't woken yet. Her body is limp, and her arm flops out of her lap.

"She's been attacked." Why I need to explain what happened is unknow. Anyone can see from the dried blood on her face she's hurt badly. "Hold on baby, hold on for me," I whisper in her ear.

Placing a kiss on her temple, I follow the receptionist into a room. There's an unmade bed inside and I place Maggie on it. The mattress is soft enough, but it doesn't feel comfortable. The room smells heavily in Clorox, at least it's clean.

A nurse rushes in pulling her stethoscope out, putting it on Maggie's chest. There are two more nurses that come in. One of them is from my last visit.

Satisfied with hearing Maggie's heartbeat, without saying anything the first nurse starts pulling out packages from a drawer while the other leaves and starts bringing equipment in.

"Her heartbeat is strong," the nurse says with her back to me. "I'm going to start her drip."

Drip?

"Are you family?"

The question throws me off. *Are you family?*

"Sir I cannot give any more information if you're not family," she must see the look on my face.

Before she can kick me out, I tell her, "I'm her

fiancé," it won't be a lie for much longer. I know without a shadow of doubt Maggie is the one I want to spend the rest of my life with. I just need her to pull through.

The nurses rush in with an IV stand, hooking Maggie up. They finish and unlock the wheels to the bed, one of them gets behind the head of the bed pushing it out.

"Wait, where are we going?" Where she goes, I go. I'm not leaving her alone with anyone.

"We're taking her to a sterile room where we'll be able to look at her head closer. She's going to need stitches or staples. We won't know until the doctor has a look. You will need to wait here."

They wheel her out, and I have to breathe in and out, in and out. The walls are growing closer with each passing second. They're not coming back to tell me she's not going home. They're not going to say she didn't make it. I keep telling myself she's going to be okay. She's not going to leave me.

Jays hand lands on my shoulder, giving it a slight squeeze. Words aren't spoken, he knows I don't handle hospitals well. I've never told anyone why, but they do know my mother is no longer with me so I can only speculate they have a guess.

What feels like hours pass by. I haven't moved from the same chair I've been sitting in since Maggie was wheeled out. I haven't even moved from the same spot where my butt has been planted.

I hear talking in the hallway, but the words are

muffle. Are they bringing her back? Did something happen?

Wheels squeak when a bed is pushed in front of me. Maggie's beautiful face is still sleeping. I rush to her, picking her hand up. I place a kiss on her pinky as I promise to always look after her. I place a kiss on her ring finger because I promise to love and cherish her. Then her middle finger because she loves to use it when she gets upset at me. Her pointed finger because she scolds me like a child and lastly her thumb.

The nurse lets us know that she will inform us when she finds out if there's any permanent damage to Maggie. We're waiting for the scans. Jay talked me into stepping out. I was reluctant but the nurses reassured me that if something changed, they would come and get me. I think they're full of shit but I'm holding them to their word.

"What do you want to do about her?" Jay asks, covering his mouth. "If you let it go, she'll just do it again."

He's right. Nat is responsible for everything. My car, Maggie almost getting ran over. I can't believe she went to the trouble of having her car wrapped to hide her identity. I'm beyond amazed on how low she went.

When I came home from the lake house, Johnny was there and explained in detail how she stole Charles' bat out of his apartment, had her car wrapped, and smashed my bar. I treated her like a sister. We grew up together. I had no idea she used

Charles to try and make me jealous. I can remember her flirting, but I always blew it off. Never considering she was a loose cannon or how my dad puts it. She's a few slices short of a full loaf. A saying he picked up from god knows where.

"Make it look good," I tell him under my breath while I cover my mouth. We don't need anyone to read our lips if we're suspected in a missing person report.

Epilogne 1

Maggie

"Please stop. I can do it myself," I tell the bulky man who won't let me do anything for myself.

"You let him help," my mom smacks my hand.

Colt kisses my mom on the cheek telling her, "Thank you Mrs. Wilson," I want to roll my eyes, but that will get me another slap.

I left the hospital a few days ago and was given the okay to return to work if I felt like it. Someone keeps blocking me from returning, saying I need to stay home to rest. Colt brings me my work home every night, and every night I tell him I'm ready to get back. There's someone upstairs in that head of his but they're not listening to my words.

His apartment is finished, and I know he's avoiding moving in to look after me. Since I'm on strict orders from Colt not to leave my apartment. I haven't seen it. A greater part of me wishes he would move in with me but I'm too chicken to ask. I know how devastated he was when his bar and apartment were vandalized. I know it would be too much to ask for him to stay.

"Colt. I can feed myself," I try to grab my fork out of his hand, but it drops on the carpet, smearing red sauce from my lasagna. I give him a face that lets him know I'm going to kill him when they leave.

My parents and sister brought dinner by. We're all sitting around my table that rarely gets put to use. It's crazy because my parents have been to my apartment only one other time and it was to help me move in.

I drop my face into my hands, trying to rub the tension out from the headache that's starting to build. *Let me make it through this day.*

Colt clears his throat and he's on one knee with a small velvet box open in his hand.

"Colt," my eyes fill with tears and my vision gets cloudy.

"Will you marry me?" his voice so soft and tender. "I can't be without you. I don't even want to try."

I look up to my family that has somehow grown to include an extra person. Connor stands beside my dad with a huge proud smile on his face.

"Maggie... do I need to beg?"

The dam opens and I let the tears rush out as I scream, "YES!" leaping forward, I wrap my arms around the only man that has ever treated me like a queen.

Epilogne 2

Colt
Two Years Later

I stand over the grave of the first woman in my life. The only woman who showed me what love and kindness was. Then I met my wife. Maggie's love is different. It showers me with her strength. It gives me a reason to get up every day to be a man. The kind of man she needs to take care of her. Now there's another girl in my life. My daughter.

Her cries vibrate my ear drums. Maggie reaches over trying to pull her back, but I don't let go. I love holding her. My hand pats her back and I bend my knees, trying to rock her.

"Shhh," I try and coach her back to sleep.

"It's her feeding time," Maggie informs me.

"Hand me her bottle," I don't want to let go. I want to hold her until she's grown and even then, I don't want to give her up.

Maggie slips the small bottle into my hand, and I let Harley lay in the crock of my arm. She's so small laying up against my chest. When she was born, I was too caught up with being frightened I would break her. She looked fragile.

Life is fragile. It's a gift that I used to take for granted. Never again. I soak up all the little moments of dirty diapers, crying nights, but most of all I soak up when Harley lays on my bare chest so I can feel her skin. The life that Maggie and I created.

"Are you ready to go?" I hand Harley to Maggie. "I'll be along in a few minutes. Go ahead and turn the car on, get the air going."

Maggie takes Harley and walks off.

I stare down at the marble tombstone. There are no tears this time, no darkness hanging over me. There's only happiness in my heart.

I inhale. Letting it out, I say, "Thank you for the life you gave me. Thank you for loving dad to the fullest. Because of you, I knew what real love was, how it looked, how it felt. Until I see you again."

I place the single white rose on top of the stone. I turn to see my wife climbing in the backseat of our new car.

"I'm one lucky man."

Acknowledgment

Thank you to my family, friends, my PA, my ARC group, readers and all the booktokers for your support. I couldn't do this without you.
I'm truly grateful and honored that anyone would take their time to help me or read one of my books. Thank you for all the care and love you have shown.

Love to all!

Aurelia

ABOUT THE AUTHOR

Aurelia writes dark and contemporary romance and enjoys reading it just as much! She lives in Alabama with her husband, daughter, and fur babies. She spends most of her time caring for her loved ones and plotting stories. She's excited to share her stories and to grow as an author. Look for more outstanding stories from Aurelia by following her on social media.